JOY IN
HIS HEART

KATE WELSH

Steeple
Hill®

Published by Steeple Hill Books™

STEEPLE HILL BOOKS

Steeple
Hill®

ISBN 0-373-87335-2

JOY IN HIS HEART

Copyright © 2005 by Kate Welsh

www.SteepleHill.com

Printed in U.S.A.

To Rita and Jean. Thanks for all the years of encouragement of my writing and the day-to-day camaraderie. I miss you both.

Because he has set his love upon Me,
I will deliver him; I will set him on high,
because he has known my name.

He shall call upon Me, and I will answer him;
I will be with him in trouble;
I will deliver him and honor him.
—*Psalms* 91:14–15

Chapter One

"**G**o away," Joy Lovell grumbled as she pulled a pillow over her head and tried to hide from the ringing
phone. But its insistent peal penetrated her consciousness and the thread of her favorite dream faded from her
reach as her answering machine greeted her caller. Joy
lay unmoving, hoping the dream would reappear and
that the caller would go away. Today was her day off.
She had no intention of moving for at least another hour.

"Come on, Lovell. I know you're there," Kip Webster's voice called to her via her answering machine.
"Pick up. I'm desperate here."

Joy groaned and pushed aside the pillow as she
reached for the phone in spite of her plans. "You'd
better be desperate about something important," she
said into the receiver, then peered at the clock on her
bedside table as she sat up, trying to kick start her brain.
"Really desperate. You interrupted a great dream. I was
in the middle of doing an air show with the Blue
Angels."

"Listen, I have a huge problem. I had an Angel Flight scheduled this morning. I'm supposed to fly a kid and his doctor up to Ogdensburg in northern New York state and bring the doc back again but I'm sick as a dog. I picked up that virus my sister's kids have been passing around. Even if I start feeling better, I shouldn't be near the patient. And you're the only one I haven't been near at Agape Air."

Joy frowned at the receiver, wakefulness taking over and letting her hear how shaky Kip's voice was. She flopped back against the pillows and thought about her commitment to Angel Flight and the sick children who needed her time. Thankfully she'd kept her plans for today to a minimum—lunch with her sister-in-law and dinner at her mother's. Neither promise compared to her commitment to the Angel Flight organization or one of the patients it served.

Joy pushed herself back to a sitting position and picked up the pen and notepad she kept next to the phone. "Who am I flying and what time were you scheduled to meet them at the field?"

Less than an hour later Joy drove through the front gate of Agape Air just as the ambulance left. She rolled down her window. "Everyone get on board okay?" she asked the driver.

"They're all set. George said your pilot got sick and that you're filling in."

She nodded but saw something in his eyes. Worry, maybe. "Is there something about this patient I need to know?"

"Nah. The kid's pretty well sedated. He only had surgery two days ago. His doc's just annoyed that you're late."

Joy grimaced, then winked at the older man. "Well, the doc will just have to get glad again, won't he? Kip didn't plan this to inconvenience anyone and he woke me out of a sound sleep not thirty minutes ago. I did my best."

"I hear ya. Have a good flight," the driver called and moved ahead. Joy shrugged and drove to her parking spot next to the hangar.

She breezed into the office. "Everything all handled, Uncle George?"

"Mornin', toots. It's all handled just like I promised." George Brady's fast, clipped speech had slowed and was slightly slurred after a recent stroke. "Plane's fine. All gassed up. Showed the doc around her and gave him all the emergency procedures. But listen, toots—"

Joy glanced at the clock over Uncle George's head, mentally calculating the trip and the return time. They really were running late. She reluctantly interrupted him. "There's no time to chat, Uncle George." She leaned over the counter to kiss his cheek after signing off on the flight plan Kip had already filed. She started for the door to the flight line. "I really have to get a move on."

"You need to know the doc is—"

"Annoyed. I know. I'll see you later tonight at Mom's," Joy called over her shoulder and pushed open the door.

"But it's—"

She couldn't hear the rest of what he said because it got mixed in with the familiar cacophony of engine noises bleeding in through the hangar door. Joy rushed out to the plane—a sweet little Cessna Caravan—and did her walk-around pre-flight inspection, then hopped into her seat and closed the door. She glanced back at her passengers. She could see the back of a white coat. The doc was turned away and bent over, examining the IV line on his patient.

Joy finished her preflight check without a word to her adult passenger. If he was in such a hurry, she wouldn't waste even a second on pleasantries. She checked the last item on her list, tucked the clipboard in the pocket next to her seat and started the engine as she radioed the tower to clear them for takeoff.

When the tower radioed the all-clear, Joy shouted over her shoulder, "Are you buckled up, doc, and is your seat locked forward?" Then she turned to check that he'd complied with her instructions.

Every platelet in her blood froze in place.

Brian Peterson. Joy took in his tall, golden, handsome frame at a glance. He sat in the specially designed pivoting rear seat in the cargo area next to where Sean Boyle lay on a strapped-down gurney.

"What are *you* doing here?" she asked in her frostiest tone, fumbling for the manifest. She checked the information Uncle George left on the seat next to her. "Zack Stevens is listed as the flight physician."

Brian's brown eyes glittered. "He's sick. I could ask you the same thing. I was told Kip Webster was the pilot."

"Kip picked up a bug, too." Joy used the time it took to toss the manifest onto the seat to regain her composure. She sucked in a deep breath before continuing. "It looks as if you're stuck with me, doctor. How's the patient?" She glanced toward the boy on the gurney.

"Sedated. He only had surgery day before yesterday, so try to keep it a smooth flight."

"Oops." She gave him a sarcastic smile. The first sign of trouble between them, twelve years ago, was Brian's refusal to fly with her. "There goes all those barrel rolls I had planned to entertain the kid. Maybe I'll get to them on the way home for your sake. Or are you still afraid of flying?"

"I was never afraid to fly. Just afraid of flying with a kid at the controls." His voice was laced with annoyance.

"Not to worry. I'm not a kid anymore. Besides I'd only go to the trouble to entertain a friend. You ceased to be one of those a long time ago."

Brian winced and settled back in his seat, pretending great concentration on the medical chart in his lap. He watched as Joy turned and focused on their takeoff. She still didn't pull her punches. That hadn't changed over the years. Her fascination with flying hadn't, either. He'd once tried to save her from the dangerous path her godfather had set her on when he'd taught her to fly. And for Brian's trouble and his marriage proposal, she'd stomped on his heart when she'd changed her mind about marrying him and gone her own way.

But that was twelve years ago. He managed to go months now without thinking about her. Consequently, even though this was her flight service and field, when he'd seen a six-foot-tall pilot approach the aircraft, he'd never considered it might be her. Even the sun glinting off the short blond hair that peeked out from under the pale blue Agape Air ball cap hadn't caused him a moment's thought. After all, Kip Webster was six foot and blond, so at a glance Brian hadn't realized the pilot was a woman, let alone Joy.

She had wide shoulders and narrow hips. And there had been that new short haircut, the dark military style sunglasses and that ball cap to throw him off. The khakis and brown leather flight jacket didn't help, either. Had she not looked so shocked by his presence on her plane, he'd have thought she'd concealed her identity until it was too late for him to change his mind about the flight. He'd never do that when a patient's welfare was involved, though. And he grudgingly admitted Joy wouldn't, either.

Remembering his mother's updates on Joy, Brian flipped through his patient's chart. It was to be expected that her name would come up every now and then. Their families were close. Their mothers talked all the time, and his brother was Joy's brother's best friend. Consequently, Brian knew more about Joy than he wanted. He knew she'd bought a house on a small parcel of land in Village Green a year ago. He knew that besides her regular work as a pilot, she occasionally flew rescue missions in her own restored Korean War era helicopter and that she dropped smoke jumpers practically on top of forest fires to fight them for a few of the state park services around the nation. He knew she practically ran Agape Air now that George Brady was semiretired after his stroke.

Brian didn't go digging for facts on her. Little facts about her seemed to naturally filter into family conversations like that she'd begun to buy out her uncle's share of the business and she would be sole owner any day.

He always managed to put her out of his mind until he saw her from afar at the hospital, or dreamed of her descending the stairs toward him the night he'd taken her to a formal high school function during the winter of her senior year. The worst times came after a family celebration too big to avoid that put them at the same event. The last occasion he saw her at was her brother's wedding. The time before that was her father's funeral. That day, he'd longed to comfort her until he'd noticed she was the only one not shedding a tear for Jimmy Lovell.

Joy had become hardened by life, but, as always, the second he caught sight of her she was back in his thoughts with a vengeance. He wondered if her clear blue eyes reflected who she'd become. From his seat, Brian watched her every move, but he could find no fault with the competence she showed at the controls as she taxied onto the runway and guided the plane into the air. He wanted to, and the immaturity of that urge shocked him. It was sour grapes and he knew it. She had chosen this difficult, dangerous and uncertain life over the one he could have given her as a doctor's wife. He'd wanted to give her an easy life without financial responsibilities or uncertainty. And instead she'd gone chasing after both. He wished he could get over his anger at her and his worry for her. Then maybe he could get on with his life.

* * *

Joy pitched the empty soda cup into the trash and stalked back to the aircraft, tucking her magazine under her arm. She checked her watch. "Sixteen hundred," she muttered aloud. That was, of course, exactly only five minutes since the last time she'd checked it. "Doctor Peterson apparently doesn't have the same problem with late schedules when he's the cause."

Because of him, she would be flying on instruments by the time they approached Agape Field. It wasn't a piloting problem but a personal one. She hated the thought of being sequestered with him inside the plane with a blanket of stars and blackness surrounding them. Night-flying set a mood of silent intimacy when two people were alone in the sky—just the two of them and the long quiet night. It was a feeling she usually enjoyed when she was with a friend. But as she'd pointed out to Brian just this morning, he was hardly a friend.

A night flight tended to promote conversation in novices as they tried to dispel the solitude of the surrounding darkness. She had a feeling world-wise Brian was a novice to small plane flight and she wished he'd get to the airfield so they could leave. The more miles they put behind them in the daylight hours, the happier she'd be.

Just then, a taxi pulled up to the gate. The guard pointed toward a recently erected shed where passengers were now screened before they were allowed near the planes. A sign and consequence of the times. But though she had no patience for Brian and his snide remarks, she knew he was no terrorist—domestic or otherwise—and they were burning daylight.

Putting her fingers between her lips, she delivered a sharp whistle in the direction of the gate. When the guard and Brian turned, she pointed her thumb toward her plane, then shot him an A-OK sign. She didn't know the guard by name, but he knew her and her Agape Air logo. He nodded and pointed Brian in her direction.

Joy had already done her preflight—three times—so she had the plane all ready to roll by the time he scurried into his seat. This time he took the one behind the copilot's chair. Her all-clear came at the same time she heard his seatbelt click into place. She didn't turn her head or speak. She just eased the little plane into the sky and banked onto the heading home.

"Do you make these flights often?" Brian asked.

So much for the daytime flight helping her escape the chitchat. "Often enough, I guess. And I let my pilots use the fleet for Angel Flights anytime we can fit them in. Why? Surprised that you and you brother aren't the only ones from the neighborhood with altruistic motives?"

"No, it's just that Angel Flights seem tame compared to rescuing climbers off the sheer face of a cliff or dropping smoke jumpers and flying those water tankers over miles of blazing forest fires. It's bad enough your brother's still out there getting shot at after your father got himself killed in the line of duty. Do you have to drive your poor mother around the bend too with all your daredevil stunts?"

Joy gritted her teeth. "Don't! I'm not getting into it with you, Brian. Mom has confidence in my flying. She knows I wouldn't do anything stupid. And my brother is a state police detective. He's hardly in the line of fire every day."

"I saw you on the evening news last month hovering that old chopper a few feet away from that cliff face. The commentator said it was so dangerous, three other pilots refused to try."

"And I was sitting with my mom watching the footage telling her what babies they were and how much the commentator had hyped up the whole thing to make news out of an everyday rescue. It was no big deal." She said and smirked. "But thanks for watching." Then just to shut him up she added, "And thanks for your concern. I didn't know you still cared."

An uneasy silence reigned for too short a time. But it wasn't Brian who broke it. It was her radio and she thanked whoever it was until she understood the meaning of the message.

"LEU 4211, this is Ogdensburg tower. We have a patch-in for you from the park service. Can you respond?"

Joy reached for the mike and responded, "Ogdensburg tower, this is LEU 4211. Go ahead."

There were the usual clicks and clacks then, "Joy, it's Russell Dempsey."

"Russ." Joy smiled. "It's been months. What have you got for me?"

"I can't believe our luck that you're in the area. I was hoping you could join a search but it looks as if you'll get there first. Can you stop at Piseco and pick up a spotter? A bunch of hikers just came across some yahoo and a boy. The yahoo was leading some sort of church camping trip. The hikers found the two of them near Rock Lake. They were both suffering from exposure and are pretty disoriented."

Joy grimaced. Not an uncommon story, but potentially deadly. She mentally shifted gears from her regular flight mentality to search and rescue as she listened to Russ.

"Near as we can gather he was leading the kids in the Silver Lake wilderness area. He went in on the Northville-Placid trail. Somehow they got lost. You know how those bushwacks are up there. Like I said, he's not making a lot of sense yet. He says they walked for days, then the kid they found him with fell into a stream swollen by last week's thunderstorms. He went in to save him and they were swept away. The rest of those kids are out there alone."

"So the bottom line is that the leader has no idea where the kids are," Joy said, knowing she sounded disgusted. "How many kids are we talking about here? And how old?"

"He had seven with him, so six are still out there. All of them are thirteen and under. Best we can put together is that they've been out there alone now for at least five days. It was supposed to be a daylong hike to a lean-to, a quick overnight then back out again. This ain't good, kiddo. And we're looking at some nasty developing weather cells moving in from the Great Lakes right now."

"I'll alter course and pick up your spotter. Maybe we can spot them before the weather moves in. I'll need you to find my passenger accommodations in Piseco." Joy glanced at her instruments as she began to change course. "Mind telling me why you only just heard these kids are missing? Where were their parents all this time?"

"Actually, all the parents are away at some sort of mission trip and out of phone range. Their pastor volunteered to look after their kids while they were gone and to take them camping. As far as we know, the parents don't know yet that their kids are missing. That's in the works now."

Brian scrambled into the seat next to her. "Isn't dropping me off to pick up someone else a waste of time? You only have a few hours of daylight left and I'm guessing less before the storm blows in. If all a spotter does is look for the kids or any sign of them through binoculars, I can do that."

She didn't even spare him a glance. "Absolutely not." As if she'd keep him with her longer than necessary. Puh-leeze!

"Why not? I have twenty-twenty vision."

She ignored him. "Banking to heading two-eight-two. My ETA at Piseco is—"

"You're wasting time!" Brian cut in while she still had the mic open.

"If your passenger's willing, it *would* save time," Russ said, clearly having overheard the good doctor.

"He's a novice. This is probably his first time in anything smaller than a 707. And I really don't want to take responsibility for his safety." Joy switched off the open mic to keep their inevitable argument private.

"I'm a big boy," Brian countered with Russ no longer privy to the conversation. "I'm responsible for myself."

"Not on my aircraft you aren't."

"Put your feelings for me aside, Joy. Think of those kids. Another night alone is what your stubbornness may cost them."

Stung, Joy realized that she mostly wanted to rid herself of Brian's overwhelming presence. She could usually ignore the most annoying of passengers but she couldn't forget Brian for even a second. She sighed, thinking of those poor kids in a position that was her personal idea of torture—sleeping in the forest below. She sighed.

Sorry, Lord. I didn't mean to be so selfish.

"Fine. But you have to realize that even if we spot them, they probably won't get out of there tonight. This isn't the Huey. Since I can't pull them out, we'd need to get a chopper in before the storms hit. Just do what I say, when I say and don't make me sorry I'm bringing you along or I just might toss you out and let you walk home!"

Chapter Two

Brian scanned the heavily forested land below, searching for any sign of human presence. Joy's friend Russ set their search area in the most likely spot the missing kids may be, since he knew Joy was fearless and would skim close to the treetops. They'd been flying over the thickening canopy for an hour and were so close Brian thought he could almost identify the species of the trees. He recognized sugar maples mixed in with white pine and every once in a while they passed over a several hundred acre patch of paper birch that tend to spring up in the wake of a forest fire throughout most of the Adirondacks.

Joy mentioned having helped put a fire out several years earlier. Even though he fought it, Brian couldn't help the anxious feeling he got in the pit of his stomach at the idea of her flying this close to raging flames. She didn't want his caring and protection, he sternly reminded himself, so why did he still long to give it?

Brian put the thought away and concentrated on the

terrain below. As she took them higher toward the peak of the mountain, sugar maple and white pine gave way to balsam firs. Their engine noise sent a black bear scurrying from a stream then later set a moose in a small clearing running, but there was no sign of the kids. They moved on to the next mountain peak as the sky darkened with the threatening storm, but they saw no sign of them.

"We're going to have to head in soon," Joy said.

"Just one more pass. Maybe if you fly a pattern headed down the slope, I'll get a different view of the terrain."

She blew out a breath, making her bangs flutter. "Don't ever call me stubborn again. Okay. You win. We'll make one more pass but get ready for a rough ride into Piseco. You've never been in a small plane in a storm have you?"

"Can't say I have," Brian admitted. Considering he'd never been in a plane no matter what size before that morning, he figured that was a large understatement.

He had no intention of volunteering the information to Joy, however. She regularly traversed the continent as if she were driving to the grocery store for milk and bread. He still remembered her sneering at him during the final argument of their big breakup. She'd called him Doctor Brain. It had stung—a remnant of his teens when she and a lot of others ridiculed him for his studiousness. And that day she'd combined it with doctor, making it a slur directed toward his dream for their future. A future, he'd realized at that moment in time, which wouldn't include her after all.

Just then a spear of lightning lit the darkening sky like fireworks on the Fourth of July. The wings of the Cessna rocked violently and the left wingtip dipped sharply. It felt as if a giant hand had pushed downward on it. Joy had only just straightened the wings again when they flew into a wall of rain that obliterated any view beyond the cockpit. Then, as if the air below the wings had disappeared, the plane dropped within inches of the treetops.

Joy put the plane into a steep climb and the engines whirred louder. "End of search. Buckle up and if you feel airsick there's a bag under your seat."

While growing up, fear in Joy's voice had been something he'd longed to hear. Today it was a quality Brian couldn't say he enjoyed at all. "Don't worry about me," he told her. "I'm not a bit sick. What's wrong? And don't tell me nothing."

"That was wind sheer. It's been known to slam a 747 into the ground. And these cross winds are blowing us off course." She reached for a dial and twisted it to 7700, then picked up the radio microphone. "Piseco T—"

Without warning, lightning speared right through the nose of the plane and Joy's instrument panel blinked, then blanked out. She slammed back in her seat and shook her head as if clearing her mind.

"What was that?" he gasped.

"Lightning." She glanced at her instrument panel. "It blew out my electronics." Brian heard a breathless quality in her voice and realized she was simply amazed at what had transpired in such a short time. She looked at him. "Uncle George showed you where the parachutes are kept and how to use them, right?"

"Uh-huh," he answered, uncertain suddenly of every life plan he'd ever made. Maybe his stomach wasn't as good as he'd thought. It suddenly struck home. They were in real trouble.

"Get into one of the chutes," Joy ordered, her eyes fixed onto the windshield. She was clearly trying to get the plane to climb but the engine didn't sound the same. Not at all the same. He couldn't imagine what kind of impact a lightning strike would have on the engine and he had no idea how much a plane depended on its electronics.

"There are emergency packs with the chutes," she went on in a scarily calm voice. "Take the red one. Strap it around your waist. You saw me unlock the cargo door when we got to Ogdensburg. Do you remember how I did it?"

"Yeah, but—"

Joy twisted the dial near the radio to 121.5 and scrabbled around for the microphone she'd dropped when the lightning struck. "There are no 'yeah buts' here, Brian. You're bailing out." He watched as she struggled with the steering. "Pay attention! The door pushes to the side like a van door. To the left. Got it! It won't be easy at this speed. You can get sucked out before you're ready, so brace yourself. Once you get the door open, you have to dive out low so you'll clear the tail. Count to ten after you're completely clear of the plane, then pull the ring on your chute that George showed you. Do you remember what it looks like?"

"I remember." He rolled out into the aisle between them and got himself to the compartment George Brady had shown him before Joy arrived at Agape Air that morning.

Was that only this morning?

With the sound of Joy calling out, "Mayday, mayday, this is LEU 4211," ringing in his ears, he wrenched the catch open on a door he'd never thought he'd need to touch. This was supposed to be a quick flight with a sick kid and home by the start of the Sixers game. A sort of mini-adventure in a life that had become too work-centered. Shaking his head at the turns the Lord allowed to enter the lives of His people, Brian grabbed two parachutes and all four of the red emergency packs. Then he stopped, closed his eyes and said a quick prayer.

He'd just turned to drag the chutes and packs forward when the wind seemed to toss the plane upward, then back down. The plane dipped and rose as if it had turned into a roller coaster. Brian hit the floor flat on his face with a painful thump.

"You all right back there?" Joy called as he gained his feet.

He said he was fine and then he heard her praying aloud for wisdom and guidance. It was rough before but it was worse now. The plane bucked and started vibrating like one of those motel mattresses he remembered from family vacations at the shore. "Do you know where we'll be when we get to the ground?"

He watched perspiration bead on Joy's forehead as she fought with the machinery. "There's no *we* in this. Just you. I'm sorry about this. But you'll be fine. Stick close to where you land and someone will be in to get you. When I land the plane, I'll try to let them know around where I dropped you."

Brian couldn't believe his ears. "*If* you land it, you mean. You could just as easily crash into a mountainside. You think I'm jumping to safety and leaving you up here fighting for your life? Did that lightning strike fry your brain?"

"Bri—"

"Don't *Bri* me. There is no way on earth I'm going to look your mother and brother in the eyes and tell them I let you save me while you stayed behind to save a hunk of metal!"

"Look, Peterson! You said you'd do as I say. Now get that cargo door open and bail!" she shouted over the rattling of the plane and rolling thunder.

Why she'd risk her life for an inanimate object, even one as expensive as a plane, boggled his mind and he intended to find out later. There would be a later for both of them, he promised himself, and he prepared to do battle. He recognized that stubborn set of her chin, but she didn't know stubborn if she thought he'd leave her behind.

He looked ahead trying to find the right words to convince her how foolish she was being and as he did the windshield was suddenly ablaze with sunlight. The storm vanished in thin air but his relief was short-lived as Joy fought a new teeth-rattling vibration.

"Oh, sweetheart," she crooned. "I don't think I can save you. There goes the rest of your oil pressure," she said, and he knew with a pang that she was talking to the plane and not him. It bothered him for a split second, but then she gave in and started giving him orders.

"It looks as if you're going to get your way. Hustle into that seat again and take the yoke. Hold it right where I leave it. I was in a climb when I lost the avionics so we're gaining altitude. And take the radio. It's already on the emergency frequency. Repeat our mayday and LEU 4211 the way I was doing. Hopefully someone out there is hearing us."

Brian's stomach roiled. "You don't know?"

"The radio may have fried when the electronics did. We aren't getting anything on it, that's for sure."

Brian looked down at the trees whizzing by far under them. She *had* gained altitude. But, sunshine notwithstanding, this plane wasn't getting them anywhere near civilization. Below was one of the roughest, most isolated areas of the Adirondacks. He reached out and grasped her forearm.

She looked at him, her blue eyes wide and worried. "What?"

"You're coming with me? You promise? You aren't just trying to fake me out?"

"I don't have a death wish, Brian," she said and stood to wrestle into the parachute and an emergency pack. Then she grabbed a map and stuffed it in the pocket of her jacket. When she took over at the controls again, her voice shook but he knew it was the vibration of the straining engine transferring through the yoke and no longer fear from brave and fearless Joy Lovell. She seemed to have gone into a mental zone where duty and skill had banished all emotion but determination.

"I'm going to keep her as high up as I can. There's no open land below so be careful of the tree canopy.

Now get that door open. And, Bri, when we go, it's going to have to be fast. When I lost the electronics, I lost my autopilot. My belt hooked around the yoke is all we'll have keeping us aloft and that won't last long. Now move it."

Joy felt the rushing air fill the plane a minute later and not a moment too soon. This bird was going down any second. Then she heard a lot of scrabbling around behind her. "I mean it! We have to go!"

Brian called back that he was ready.

"Okay, go. I'm right on your six," she called back to him, then took a deep breath and let go of the jury-rigged yoke.

It held.

Joy didn't stick around to see how long it would. She just pivoted out of the seat and ran, diving out the doorway toward the ground. As she'd advised Brian, she waited until the count of ten before yanking the cord, and got ready for the inevitable jerk of the parachute catching the air. The open parachute dragged her higher than the crippled plane that had already passed by her.

She scanned the terrain below. They were deep in the wilderness preserve in an area she didn't think she'd ever flown over before. It was terribly obvious at that moment that they'd been blown way off course. Though still in the state park they were far off the beaten path where few humans ever strayed.

Mentally she created a survival checklist beyond the obvious emergency packs she and Brian had around their waists. They'd need to make their way to the crash site. She looked around trying to memorize what she was seeing so she could pinpoint the landmarks on the map, then glued her gaze on the plane. The transponder would draw the rescue planes right to them if they were near the plane. Getting to the wreckage would have to be their first priority.

But she had to make sure she landed near Brian, so she twisted until she saw his chute floating below. He'd caught a different current of wind than she was riding. She pulled on her guide wires to close the widening distance between them as they floated toward earth. Once she was sure they were on the same basic track toward the ground, she turned her attention back to the plane.

Surprised and chagrined, Joy saw the plane catch an updraft and bank onto an altered heading. It had remained aloft for much longer than she'd anticipated, especially considering her makeshift autopilot. Finally, the tail rose and sent the beautiful blue-and-white craft skimming gracefully toward the ground, but it dropped altitude slowly and headed in the direction of a different mountain peak from the one where she and Brian would most likely land.

Still, it didn't drill downward but drifted straight into a hole in the trees' canopy, then disappeared miles away. She continued to watch, hoping she'd dumped the right amount of fuel to keep it from exploding on impact. She breathed a sigh of relief when no smoke rose over the dense woodlands.

So intent was she on watching for the crash site, though, that Joy didn't see trouble rushing up to meet her. It was as if the tentacles of a giant wooden octopus reached into the air and snatched her off course. Her feet cracked into the monster, her ankle buckled and her knee twisted as she slammed into the beast. Pain exploded in her head, then her shoulder, as her open chute caught the wind and dragged her sideways away from one monster and into the arms of another. Then another. And then the world went black with the sound of cracking, breaking branches accompanying each new flash of pain.

"Joy! Yo, Joy. Come on. Quit clowning around and answer me."

Joy heard Brian's demand for an answer from the end of a long, dark tunnel she found herself wandering through. It was filled with a thick fog or maybe Jell-O. She wasn't sure what it was that made her feel nearly weightless, as if she were bobbing and drifting toward the surface.

Wait a minute! Why is Brian Peterson anywhere near me? And how did we get in this tunnel in the first place?

She tried to move but her arms and legs appeared to be tied down even though she was nearly sure her body was floating. Definitely floating.

And who had tied her up?

All at once the memory of recent events collided with the confusion in her brain, and her mind cleared. Almost of their own accord her eyes popped open. Joy groaned and winced as the setting sun drilled into her brain through her eyeballs. She slammed her eyelids shut again but it was too late to retreat.

She was awake now. Wide awake.

It didn't take a genius to realize what had happened.

Especially since there was a harness holding her weight and it hung from a tangle of lines. Eyes still closed, Joy tried to slow her pounding heart.

She carefully cracked her eyelids open again and took stock of her situation. Slowly she pivoted her head downward. She was a good seventy feet off the ground and tangled in some of her lines and the branches of a tree.

Starting with her fingers and toes, Joy moved each extremity. Tensed each muscle group. Counted her injuries. Her right ankle was sprained or broken. Her right knee, too. Her hands and elbows seemed to be okay but her left forearm stung. That shoulder was out of commission, too, but in a way she couldn't quite grasp. All she knew was nothing had ever hurt quite the way her shoulder did.

Then she looked up and added another injury to the growing list. Judging from the pain in her head, dizziness and the fact that she'd apparently been napping high in a tree while hanging from some pretty thin branches, Joy figured she probably had at least a mild concussion, too.

What made things even more dicey was that she was scared spitless. Oh, not of the tenuous hold she had on safety hanging in a tree but of all that wilderness below and around her. She was still the big, stupid 'fraidy-cat she'd been as a girl after watching *The Wizard of Oz*. The dark forest and poor Dorothy's trek through it had been her worst childhood nightmare. It had been the threat of lions and tigers and bears, and not the wicked witch, that used to have her screaming in the night. She looked around and refused to think about those flying monkeys.

Joy Lovell—pilot extraordinaire—was afraid of the wide open spaces she usually soared over as she was of nothing else in the world.

Even death.

Brian's call from below dragged Joy from her fear-induced musings. But the situation didn't get better with examination. She was stuck good and proper, and Brian Peterson, her ex-fiancé, was her only hope of getting down in one piece.

She searched her mind for an alternative to asking for his help. Unfortunately, no ideas came to mind other than just keeping quiet and starving to death in a tree. The idea had a certain amount of merit, she thought wryly.

After all, this was the man who'd valued her and her goals so little that he'd expected her to give up her dreams to play Little Susy Homemaker to his Doctor Brain. This was the man who couldn't wait for her while she established a career in her chosen field while he was engrossed in medical school. This was the man who'd made her hope that she'd actually found someone who had accepted her for herself. But he had turned on a dime and demanded that she mold herself into someone who would be his image of the ideal doctor's wife—someone she couldn't be.

This was the man who'd broken her heart.

Then there was her responsibility for the entire situation to consider. It was her fault Brian was out there and in danger. She should never have given in to his demand that she include him. She'd known he'd be safer at Piseco than on a search and rescue mission. She *never* second-guessed herself! Why had she done it this time?

Now she was going to have to risk his life further. He'd talked about not wanting to face her mother and brother if she hadn't managed a safe landing. She looked at the distance separating them. He could easily fall while climbing the tree. And if he fell rescuing her, she'd have to face *his* parents and brother. Did he think that would be any easier for her just because he happened to be male? She was the one in charge. The one responsible for his safety.

Still, she didn't see how she could cut herself loose. She couldn't even raise her left arm. And even if she could cut and unbuckle herself and get loose of the chute, there was still the long climb to the ground with only one good arm and one good leg, thanks to her injuries. "And let's not forget a brain that feels like it's made of pudding," she muttered just before realizing her left hand felt wet and sticky. She looked down and noticed for the first time that blood flowed from somewhere on her forearm under her jacket sleeve.

Just then a scuffling sound from below drew her attention. "Joy!" Brian called.

She rolled her eyes. Since dying out here wasn't now, nor had it ever been, an option, it looked as if Doctor Brain was her only hope.

Great! She groaned. Just great!

Chapter Three

Brian cupped his hands around his mouth. "Joy." His voice was nearly gone from calling her name. Fear choked him. Fear for her. She was a royal pain in the neck but he couldn't think of the world without her in it—somewhere. Panic overwhelmed him. If she'd jumped why couldn't he find her? He should never have left her in that plane with only a promise that she'd follow. But she'd been so convincing.

Please, Lord, let her be safe. Let me find her.

"I'm up *here*."

Brian snapped his head upward toward Joy's muffled but annoyed voice and found a sight he'd never even considered. Joy Lovell trussed up like a Christmas turkey high in a tree. He laughed and the tension that had been building in him drained just seeing her safely on the ground. Well, not exactly on the ground but he'd been close to believing she'd lied—that she hadn't intended to jump at all.

"Forget to watch where you were going?" he teased,

reveling in overwhelming relief that she wasn't in the air fighting for her life and that stupid plane. "You really ought to take your own advice. You know? 'Watch out for the trees' I think you said."

"I was trying to track the plane to the ground, idiot," Joy shouted down at him. He grinned at the escalating annoyance in her tone. He figured if there was a way to shout through gritted teeth, she had.

Relief washed over him. Joy was all right. What was that old saying he'd once heard from her uncle? "Any landing you walk away from was a good one." Brian had to add, "any crash you walked away from wasn't too bad, either."

Though her obsession with saving that plane nearly overshadowed his relief. He forced the troubling thoughts away, once again promising himself to take it up with her later. "Why? I understand that you were attached to the plane but it isn't going to help us get home. I think that had better be our priority, don't you?"

"Actually it *could* help us get rescued. Right now, though, I have a bigger problem. This isn't funny, Peterson," she shouted. "I can't get myself free."

So she might actually have to admit to needing his help? He was pretty sure that hadn't happened to Joy in years—if ever. Oh, this was nearly worth the price of admission. And, considering that the price had been diving out of that plane and floating to the ground under a glorified umbrella, Brian really thought he deserved a little fun. "You're stuck? Leave your Swiss Army knife at home, Joyless?" he chided, using an old nickname he knew really bugged her.

"No! I have my knife in a pocket but I did something indescribably nasty to my shoulder and arm. If I could cut myself loose, I'd fall because I also sprained or broke my right knee and ankle.... Oh, and don't make yourself sick laughing over this one, but if all that isn't enough fun, I think I've got a concussion, too."

Brian stared up at her for a protracted moment, waiting for one of her usual one-line zingers that were always designed to make him feel like a fool for believing one of her wild tales. She'd been suckering him since she was just out of diapers.

But this time she didn't follow up with a single word. His stomach sank. "You aren't kidding, are you?" he asked, feeling like a first-class creep. He'd let old hurts and rivalries goad him into betraying his Hippocratic oath.

"No, Doctor *Brain,* I'm not kidding. And the really sad thing is, I have to depend on you and you've probably never climbed a tree in your life. How's that for the end of a perfect day?"

Now it was Brian's turn to grit his teeth. He let the Doctor Brain moniker slide. He'd started this round of nastiness after all. But why did she always have to make him sound like a bumbling weakling?

He slowly circled the tree, looking at it, all the while feeling her eyes on him. "I *have* climbed trees, Joy. In fact, I was quite good at it." The first branch was over twelve feet off the ground and the first thirty feet of the branches were spread pretty far apart. "I need to tie the lines from my chute together and use it to scale the main trunk before I can get anywhere near you," he told her.

"There's a rope with a grappling hook in your emergency pack. One in mine, too," she said, then after some awkward twisting and turning, she managed to toss her rope to the ground. "Can you hurry?" she added softly. The soft winded sound of her voice shook Brian. Joy never used that tone of voice. The exertion and pain of unpacking the rope must have worn her out.

Brian cringed, feeling like an idiot for having goaded her. But then, feeling like that around Joy was nothing unusual. No one on earth had ever gotten to him the way she could. But this time it wasn't her fault. He was the one who'd made light of her situation. Why hadn't he assumed she'd have injuries since she'd obviously crashed into a tree?

But he knew why. Though he forgot about it each and every time she scared a year off his life, he'd always seen her as indestructible. Believing that got him through every wild story her brother ever told him about her escapades. Brian frowned and looked back up at Joy hanging limply in the tree. Maybe she was more fragile than he'd ever realized.

Troubled by his rapidly changing perspective of Joy, Brian quickly unpacked his rope, then tossed the pack next to the parachute, followed by the bundle he'd managed to carry with him from the plane.

He had never used a grappling hook but he managed to hook it to the first branch on the third try. From there to the next level of branches was just as far but he quickly climbed it. His hands, blistered and bleeding, would take some time to heal but he reached Joy ten minutes after starting his climb. Of course, he'd had to endure a critique of his technique from the moment he entered Joy's line of sight. She'd made a few good suggestions, but that didn't make her guidance of his rescue any easier to take.

"I don't think that branch will hold you," Joy said when Brian went to move onto the branch he needed to traverse in order to cut the lines tangled with her arm.

"Yes, it will," he said as he gingerly walked the narrowing branch. "You know, you make a really lousy damsel in distress. This is my rescue. Would you just let me do it my way?"

"Sorry. Maybe I'm out of damsel practice. Oh, no. Wait. It could be because I've never needed someone to rescue me."

"Well, you need one now. I'm sorry it's me, but it is, so relax and stop nattering at me. I'm using the branch above to support some of my weight. Now shush."

Her blue eyes blazed. "Don't 'shush' me. I'm getting rescued so I get to help. And I don't natter. You have to be at least sixty to natter."

Brian had to grin. "Is that a rule I don't know about?" he asked, hoping a little nonsensical conversation would calm both their nerves as he made his way to her. Now that he'd reached her level he saw damage to at least three other trees, which meant she'd been dragged through them. He sincerely prayed the injuries she'd already catalogued were all that was wrong with her. He caught his breath when he saw that a branch had punctured the pack at her waist. If it had gone all the way through....

She was lucky to be alive.

"Now let's see what the problem is with your knee and ankle," he said, his voice unsteady even though he was on a relatively stable footing next to her.

She glared at him. "Look, just get me free. I didn't ask you up here to play doctor."

Insulted, he snapped, "I *am* a doctor, Joy. I don't play at it. Not now and not ever in my life."

The fire in her eyes banked a little and she looked away. "I still don't need you doctoring me. I probably exaggerated my injuries anyway. My head feels better now that I've been conscious for a while and I'm sure my knee and ankle are just slightly sprained. In fact, I'm sure I can get down on my own if you cut me free."

Brian sighed. She was determined to make this just as difficult as possible, even though one look and he knew her shoulder was dislocated. The longer it stayed out of joint the harder it would be to get it back where it belonged and the longer her recovery would be. And since she'd been unconscious there was a good bet she'd been right to guess she might have at least a slight concussion. Her leg was so badly hurt, too, that she winced whenever she tried to move it. Sure it would hold her weight! For 2.2 seconds before she plummeted to the ground.

"You think you can climb down? You can hardly move." He got nothing but a dirty look in response. "Ever read Proverbs 16, Joy?" he demanded after she remained stubbornly silent. "Verse 18 warns that 'Pride goes before destruction and a haughty spirit before a fall.' The way you're acting I'd say it was written just for you." He pointed downward. "And that is one long fall! Now listen. I'm going to get you down—*my way.* Using your harness. You can't climb and I admit to not being strong enough to get down with you on my back."

She opened her mouth but he wasn't going to cling to a branch arguing all day or give her another chance to try sticking pins in his ego. "We both aren't happy with being stuck out here together," he told her. "But we are. There's too much anger and resentment between us. It's going to get in the way of us relying on each other. We're going to need to do that to survive. So please just take my hand and pray with me before we make a mess of this whole thing."

He reached out and took her right hand. He took a deep cleansing breath before he began. "Lord, I beg Your forgiveness for not thinking to ask Joy if she was hurt before I started us on the path to yet another argument. We thank You for our deliverance from certain death in the plane. We beg Your help again. Please teach us how to deal fairly and patiently with each other now that You've graciously spared us. We also pray for those children who are out here somewhere alone and afraid. Comfort them this night, Lord, and help us all find our way back to our loved ones. Do you want to add anything?" he asked Joy.

"No, that was fine," she said, her tone much different. "Thanks for thinking of it." She looked away but not before Brian saw the uncertain expression in her eyes. It was obvious she absolutely hated feeling helpless. "So what's the plan, boy genius?" she asked, looking toward the ground.

"There is a good sturdy branch a few yards above us

so I thought we'd put it to good use. I can tie your harness to the rope, cut you loose from the chute, then lower you to the ground using the branch as a makeshift pulley."

"But then you'll still be up here. And I'll be down there."

Brian stared at her. He couldn't imagine what she was getting at. "And your point is?" he asked, keeping his tone light even as he fought annoyance. He'd gotten up to her. He could get down much more easily, especially without her running commentary on his climbing technique.

"No point. No point at all," she said still avoiding eye contact but, even so, he could see that somehow it was he who'd scored a point. And he hadn't even tried. In fact, he didn't have a clue how he had. It bothered Brian in a way he wouldn't have suspected it could. Maybe because before that moment, if someone had asked, he would have said he knew everything important there was to know about Joy.

Now he realized he just might not know anything at all about her. It wasn't the time to explore that now though but, like her reluctance to leave the plane, he promised he'd find out later. So with nothing left to say for the moment, Brian squeezed Joy's uninjured shoulder and graced her with a serving of his best bedside-manner smile. "It'll all work out," he promised.

He'd meant what he'd said in his prayer. They needed to work together—to lean on each other. If they continued to shoot barbs at each other, that wouldn't happen. And—worst-case scenario—someone could die.

"I'll be right behind you," he found himself reassuring the most self-assured person he'd ever met. "Just the way you kept your promise to me up there when you jumped after me. Okay? You don't have to worry about standing once I get you down. I'll tie your harness off a couple feet from the ground so you don't have any weight on your leg and I'll help you out as soon as I get down."

He didn't wait for a reply but got straight to work securing her harness with the length of rope from her pack. Next he started cutting and untangling her lines, then adding them to the length of rope. Then he started the arduous task of lowering her to the ground. There was no straight path down so she had to carefully pick her way through the thickening spring foliage with only one good arm and one good leg.

She made a few startled gasps along the way that he assumed were a result of sudden pain, but soon she called up that she was within feet of the ground and he tied off the rope. Then she added that she would unlatch her harness so he could let the rope fall to the ground in case they needed it later.

He saw the wisdom behind her actions but it annoyed him that she couldn't seem to stand to let him take care of her. Knowing she was probably resting on his chute, however, let him do something else while he was up there. The parachute material caught high up in the maple called to him. If those storms came back or new ones blew in, they'd be thankful for the shelters he could build for each of them from the chutes. So he climbed higher into the thinning branches and grabbed it. About ten minutes later he dropped to the ground next to her, startling her awake.

"You took your sweet old time," she groused.

Joy looked up at Brian towering over her, her chute material bundled under his arm. He was handsome. She had to give him that. He now wore a navy-blue cotton bomber-style jacket over a white T-shirt and well-worn jeans, having shed his white doctor's coat while in Ogdensburg. Brian didn't look much like Doctor Brain, with perspiration misting his forehead and dirt smeared on one of his high cheekbones. He was more nimble and resourceful than she would have thought, too. After having grabbed his upper arm earlier to steady herself when he'd cut her loose, she now knew he had quite a lot of muscle definition in his arms.

No. Brian didn't come across as a nerdy brain now. In fact, he looked entirely too masculine and competent for her peace of mind. And that was ridiculous considering she was totally panic stricken over their circumstances and in need of someone exactly like the man Brian had turned out to be.

If only it wasn't Brian, everything would be a lot more bearable. She wondered if he had any inkling how afraid she was at that moment. He didn't seem to. That made it easier not to hate him for looking so competent while she lay helpless, hiding her fear of their surroundings and her pain, as well.

Left with a feeling of internal disquiet over her rapidly changing perceptions of him, Joy endured a quick, efficient exam, holding tears at bay. But it took every ounce of strength she could summon. Over and over she repeated the command her father had given her at age nine.

He'd come across her crying because one of the boys in the neighborhood had teased her. "Never let them see you cry," he'd told her. "Never give anyone that power over you. You're Jimmy Lovell's kid. You don't cry. Ever."

And she never had. Not once in all the twenty-one years since. Not even when he was killed in the line of duty. She'd been what her father had wanted her to be. A rock for her mother and brother.

Brian cut her khaki pants open at the seam to just above her knee, wrapped that injured joint and her ankle, then made a big deal out of shining a light in her eyes and doubling the ache in her head. Had her mother not gone to so much trouble trying to make a lady out of her, she might have slugged him for it. Or for the stupid doctor noises he kept making. She assumed they were supposed to show he cared, especially as he helped her out of her jacket, but Joy didn't believe he cared for a second. Behind that fake frozen smile, she knew he was gloating over her getting hurt and needing his help.

Added to all that, his touch, when not causing her pain, set her nerves on edge with a flood of memories. They were memories of another time and place when his touch held deep meaning and the promise of love and commitment.

"Joy, about your shoulder," he said, finally giving up on his nonverbal communication. "It's dislocated."

"Finally some good news," she quipped. But Brian just grimaced. "It is good news, isn't it? It's not broken after all. Right?" She held her breath. Any more bad news just might push her over the edge into a quivering blob of crying woman. How disgusting was that?

"It's a good news/bad news sort of injury," Brian explained.

Which of course didn't explain anything at all. "I'm up for some good news right now."

"The concussion seems to be pretty slight. The sprains are only about a level two, which isn't too bad considering how much worse it could have been."

Now what was the good doctor dancing around? "Nice. What about the shoulder? And tell me in non-doctor speak," she demanded. "You're starting to get on my nerves."

"Only starting?" He raised an eyebrow and grinned but the underlying tenseness in his body language worried her. "Okay, here it is in a nutshell," he went on. "You'll get over it a lot faster than you would a break."

"That's the good news, right? Hit me with the bad news and quit stalling."

"I've got to get it back in joint. Right now. And it's going to hurt. A lot. And the cut on the lower arm has to be cleaned and stitched. Since you do have a concussion, however slight, I'm not comfortable giving you any painkillers just yet. Tomorrow maybe, but not till then. By then more damage will be done to the shoulder if we don't fix it now. The cut can't be left open in this environment, either."

"Terrific." She sighed. It just got better and better. "Then I guess you should get at it," she told him and steeled herself for more playacting. She'd just go somewhere else the way she had when she'd crawled onto the parachute and actually managed to sleep for a few minutes. She'd put the bugs, the owl who'd scared her half to death while he was lowering her, and all the other animal noises out of her head. Out of her universe.

Brian only grimaced in response to her suggestion that he proceed.

"What's the holdup?" she snapped when he didn't just do it.

"It's just that I've seen men pass out from the pain of having a shoulder yanked back into joint."

Insulted, she huffed out a breath. "I don't faint, Brian. Just get on with it."

So he grasped her arm carefully, sending a shiver up her spine. She gritted her teeth as he started pulling, welcoming the pain. It would chase away that confusing feeling his touch seemed to spark. Then, as he braced his stockinged foot against her rib cage below her armpit, she held her breath. The cut below her elbow started to burn as he pulled on her arm. Then....

Joy hadn't known a brain could actually explode from an overload of pain. Nor had she ever believed that old saw about seeing stars. But for the second time in one lousy afternoon, she did.

When she woke a second time to Brian's concerned frown, she promised herself she'd never forgive him. Oh, not for fixing her shoulder, which she had to admit felt much better, but for having seen her faint. How humiliating was that!

Chapter Four

Joy glared at Brian, who sat next to her holding her wrist and staring at his watch. He looked concerned and oh-so-doctorly.

He looked up at last. Surprise widened his honey-brown eyes. "Oh. Back to the land of the living, I see. How do you feel?"

"You hurt me," she accused and hated the disappointment that crept into her voice.

"I'm sorry," he said. "I did try to warn you, but the good news is that I managed to clean and stitch the cut while you were still unconscious."

He was entirely too comfortable with his role and way too competent for her liking. She didn't want to talk to him or even look at him, and she certainly didn't want to move, so she turned her head to survey her surroundings. Brian had sorted all the emergency items that had been in the packs. They'd contained an awful lot more than she would have thought. Then she noticed for the first time that he had his medical bag, the pad from the gurney and even the sheets and blankets. She'd been too busy jury-rigging the yoke to watch what was going on behind her. Now she understood all that moving around behind her. Apparently he'd been planning ahead. Way too competent. She was bound to come off looking like a first-class idiot to his boy genius sooner or later. That knowledge put her on the offensive.

"Did you leave anything on the plane that wasn't nailed down?"

He shrugged. "I took a chance and tossed all the emergency provisions and anything I thought we could use into the sheet from the gurney and tied it into a bundle. I held on to it when I jumped."

"Since you cut my pant leg, I'm hoping you tossed my overnight bag too."

"The contents of both of ours, actually. I figured we might need the change of clothes and such. I mean we wouldn't have any of it or the blankets and the provisions in the extra packs if I didn't try. We really had nothing to lose. And you never know what'll come in handy, especially with those kids down here somewhere. I dropped the bundle before I hit the ground." He frowned. "I was a lot farther from you than I thought I'd be."

Ah, something she was on top of. "The plane banked and you'd drifted with the wind. I tried to glide in your direction but then I had to switch my attention back to the plane."

He grimaced, no doubt remembering that she had crashed into the trees because she'd been watching the plane's descent. "So, how do you feel?" he asked.

"Like some ham-handed man tried to pull my arm off," she snapped, refusing to admit that he'd helped her. "How am I supposed to feel?"

"I imagine grateful is too much to ask?" he drawled.

"Will you settle for glad it's over?"

Brian stood and nodded. "It'll have to do for now. Are you thirsty?"

Her mouth felt like a desert. "A little."

He walked to a capped, half bottle of water lying with his other booty and retrieved it. "Here, let me help you sit up," he said, unperturbed by her foul mood. She guessed to a doctor used to screaming children, her foul mood was no big deal.

After going down on one knee, he supported her back and helped her sit. It was awkward, as her knee was too painful to bend but she managed when he handed her the water.

"I'll immobilize the arm in a sling. It should make it a lot more bearable and the sling should remind you not to use it. It'll heal faster if you don't aggravate it with a lot of movement."

"Sure. Whatever. You're the doctor. Have you tried your cell phone?"

"I'm not getting a signal."

She hadn't thought he would. She reached for her own satellite phone and noticed for the first time it was gone from its case on her belt. Her heart sank. Had she lost it?

He picked up a mangled hunk of plastic and held up her smashed phone. "Yours didn't survive. I guess it happened when you hit the tree." He frowned. "One of the trees."

That must be why her left hip felt bruised. She thought of the map that had been in her left jacket pocket and winced when she moved her left shoulder. As she tried to reach for it, Joy winced again for another reason altogether. Her hand encountered a torn pocket.

"What hurts?" he asked.

She was already thoroughly sick of him assessing her every breath. "Nothing. Somehow I lost the map. You didn't find it, did you?"

The expression on his face was no less pained. "No. It could be anywhere. From the damage up in the trees, I think you were dragged through a few. I'm worried about the possibility of internal injuries. It must have taken quite an impact to smash your phone that completely."

"Nothing hurts but my leg and shoulder. Really," she assured him. She didn't want him poking and prodding her again. His touch, no matter how impersonal, brought back too many memories, as did his concern. And those were memories she didn't need resurrected.

"Good. Sprains and cuts I can deal with out here. I'll set up a shelter and hike to the top of this peak and try getting a signal. I'll call for help and get back as soon as I can."

He wanted to leave her? Alone? He must really hate her. She shook her head wondering why she cared and was immediately sorry. Her headache got worse, her stomach turned over and the movement pulled the muscles surrounding her shoulder. Brian was there immediately, folding the gurney pad in three and stuffing it behind her so she could recline against it. But worse was her rolling stomach and she didn't think it had a thing to do with her injuries. No. It was fear churning up her insides. Paralyzing, incapacitating, obdurate fear. He couldn't leave her out here alone. He just couldn't!

"Not up the mountain," she objected. She'd think this through. She would reason with him. Show him practical reasons why he had to do what she said. "We have to go down this one and back up the one the plane hit."

"Are you crazy? Why would you want to do that?"

She sighed. They were destined to fight into eternity! That's all there was to it. "Look, Brian, you stick to your expertise and I'll stick to mine."

He sent her a smart-aleck grin. "Oh, you're an expert in crash etiquette? How may crashes have you had anyway?"

She decided this time it would be she who wouldn't rise to the bait. "None, but that doesn't mean I don't know procedure. I've been up there looking for survivors often enough and I've taken a few refresher courses in survival that included crash etiquette, as you put it. I know what we have to do."

She seemed to have his attention so she went on. "Every aircraft carries a transponder that sends out a signal when it crashes. Searchers use the signal to find the downed plane. Because of that, the first rule in a crash is to stay with the aircraft and wait for rescue. The transponder should be drawing rescue planes or choppers. We have to get there. We have to make sure it's working and, if it is, we'll be there to be rescued. If it was damaged in the crash or from that lightning strike, we need to get it working so we can be rescued."

Brian was still listening intently and she wasn't about to lose her advantage so she continued. "Another rule is not to separate the downed party. You and I are the downed party. So you aren't going off alone. We have to stick together and get to the crash site *together*," she reiterated, pinning him. Holding his gaze.

He shook his head and looked away. "You'd never make it."

"Watch me. You aren't going without me. Besides there are six kids out here somewhere. We have a better chance of finding and getting them to safety if we're together. If they saw the plane go down they may try to get to it thinking there may be adult survivors who can help them."

Brian pursed his lips. "There has to be some kind of compromise we can reach on this," he said after a thoughtful pause. "I guess you're right about the plane, but didn't you say you thought we were being blown off course?"

"Yes, but we'd have been visible from a wide area as we came down. There's a chance they saw us, we can't discount that."

"If that's true, there's another possibility to consider," he added. "If they saw our chutes, they may be headed here. Unless we're here, they'll miss us. I could go for the plane and you could rest here."

Panic filled her once again. "You aren't leaving me behind! No way!" She took a calming breath when she noticed how closely Brian was eyeing her. She repeated her father's prime directive. *Never let them see you cry, never let them see you sweat.*

"You don't know how to diddle with a transponder to get it up and running if it isn't sending out a signal," she told him. "Uncle George taught me a few tricks. You don't even know what a transponder looks like." She nearly sighed in delight at her brilliance. There, watch him wiggle out of that one.

Brian nodded. "Okay. I see your point. How about this? I'll build each of us our own shelter here, for tonight. That way you can rest and if the kids are on this mountain and headed our way, they'll have the chance to find us here. In the morning, you should be able to take a little pain medication. It ought to help. Then, if you're up to giving it a try, we'll pack up and see if you can travel."

"I'll be up to it. Don't worry," she promised. If it got her away from Brian, bears and bugs, she just might find a way to fly herself there.

"Do you think I should light some sort of signal fire in case a search plane flies over?"

A fire? Didn't that scare away animals? "They may not send out anyone else tonight, especially after what happened to us. Just because it isn't raining here now doesn't mean those storm cells aren't all around us. But, if the storms have moved out of the area and Search and Rescue does send out searchers, they might see a fire if it was big enough. You—you can make a fire?"

He grinned. "An old Boy Scout like me? Of course I can."

Joy thought back and frowned. "I don't remember you being in Scouts."

Brian stiffened and Joy felt a little better about her

stupid fears. She'd always been good at finding his weak spots. She knew she should feel proud of that, but it was an unfortunate fact.

"I was. For about three meetings. Then I had to get a uniform or quit. My dad said if he spent the money, I had to stay in till I outgrew it or it wore out. I decided I'd rather play the piano."

Joy gave him a pitying look and raised a sarcastic eyebrow. "Of course you did," she said having loaded her voice with all the derision she could muster.

Brian stood and propped his hands on his hips. He sounded utterly disgusted when he said, "Well, at least you didn't disappoint me. It's nice to know I still know what to expect from you. I'll see what I can do about coming up with something you can use as a crutch. You know what's really sad? I never wanted you for an enemy." He shook his head sadly. "I'll get on those shelters. Hopefully the solar blankets from the emergency packs will work as water proofing because I doubt the storms are over."

He looked up toward the sky and she followed his gaze, needing to look away from the strong column of his throat—to forget that tired sadness she'd heard in his voice and saw in his eyes.

It was hard to see the sky clearly through the canopy of the forest. She hadn't realized the trees had progressed this far into leaf. The sky beyond the barrier of bright, spring green looked like a vast gray blanket that had settled over the woodlands.

"It'll probably rain again but that may be an advantage. It'll keep the bug population down, especially this early in the year."

That sounded good but what about the animals? "You were going to build a fire. What about the fire?"

"First things first. Shelter, then fire. We have blankets to keep us warm, but only if we're dry. If I start on the fire and it rains, we'll get soaked, be cold and the fire will just go out anyway."

She stared at him. True, she had taken survival courses but they didn't seem to be helping now that the real thing stared her in the face. "How do you know all this stuff?"

"My dad had a cabin in the Poconos. We didn't go there after my brother Tommy died but Dad took us up there all the time before that. Your brother, Jim, came along a few times. Remember?"

Oh, she remembered all right. And she'd been furious. It was the first taste of the men-only club she'd been fighting ever since. Jim had been the only one who could console her. And he'd done that by telling her stories about the spiders and animal sounds inside the cabin that he'd heard all night. After that, she'd been thankful for her nice city bed.

But being excluded had still chafed. Her father had always told her she had a contrary nature. Maybe he'd been right, since sleeping in a bug-filled cabin in the wilderness was her idea of torture and yet she'd still resented having been left behind. She guessed it was the not being asked that bothered her.

Brian watched the myriad emotions float across Joy's features and wished he knew exactly what she was thinking. But though he could usually guess her responses, he'd never understood their origins. Never understood her.

She slumped down against the gurney pad and closed her eyes. "So I'll finally benefit from being the only kid left home those weekends. Goody, goody. Wake me when you need your chute for your shelter."

Dismissed, Brian turned away and got to work. He'd once read about how Native Americans built shelters from branches, so he got to work selecting thin poles and thinner green branches to weave into a grid that would support the parachute material. He thanked God for the parachute line he'd salvaged as he lashed together the poles and finished the first shelter. He used the parachute material as a floor over a thick bed of dried leaves, then he flipped the rest of the chute up and over the top to form a roof and sides of the shelter. It would make an adequate wind break especially since there was enough excess to allow material to hang across the front opening. He stretched the solar blanket over the top and tied it down to guard against the rain.

Brian stood back and admired his handy work for a moment. It was small but they would be out of the elements. With the first shelter finished, he started on the poles for the second, then went to wake Joy when he was ready to use the parachute. Only then did he realize she'd been watching him. He could have sworn the look on her face said she'd been afraid he'd go off and leave her.

He shook his head and walked toward her. How could he have allowed this much animosity to grow between them? She sat up, her posture slightly defensive, then she tossed the gurney pad to the ground next to her and inched carefully onto it.

"You should have rested," he said.

"I thought with a concussion I was supposed to stay awake."

"No. I'm supposed to wake you and ask you some tricky question like who the president is or what month you were born. But I can see you're doing fine. I'll be done with your shelter in a few minutes, then you can crawl in and rest while I get the fire going."

She pointed to the completed shelter. "But that was my parachute. Why isn't that my shelter?"

"Because your chute was ripped and that was the first one I've ever built. This one will be better and have less chance of leaking wind." He held up his hand. "And before you go all feminist on me, you're hurt so you get the better shelter. You may be the pilot in charge of fixing the transponder but I'm the doctor in charge of fixing you."

He was surprised when she let the comment slide. She only said, "Can't I do something to help you? I feel guilty just sitting here watching you do all the work."

"Get stronger so we can start out in the morning," he ordered, then picked up a few of the energy bars he'd found in the emergency packs. He walked toward her and held up some of the bars. "And to that end—dinner. Peanut butter, oatmeal raisin or caramel nut?"

"I'm not very hungry."

"But you have to eat." He tossed the peanut butter bar to her and she tried to catch it with her right hand but she was a southpaw and it bobbled into her lap. "I seem to remember peanut butter being a favorite flavor of yours. Try to eat. You have to keep your strength up."

She looked down at the energy bar and nodded.

Brian found Joy asleep when he came back after finishing the shelter and building a fire between the two structures. He let her sleep and ate one of the bars before setting about making her some kind of crutch. She'd have to take care of personal needs soon and he knew she'd hate it if he had to help get her to somewhere more private.

He located the perfect branch and cut it with the cable saw he'd found in the pack. After that, he worked on the crutch for quite a while, padding the top and hand-hold with torn strips of the sheet he'd used to bundle up the items he carried from the plane. Darkness was already falling when he finished. Though he'd worked hard to make it as comfortable as he could, Brian still didn't see how she thought she was going to hike down a mountain side and then back up another in her shape.

He woke her a little while later and gave her some of the rations he'd heated up. While she went off alone after eating, Brian tucked the gurney pad and blanket inside her shelter, then helped her inside when she'd returned.

Feeling the need to fill in the awkward silence that once again settled between them, Brian tried making small talk about the beauty of God that surrounded them. He wondered aloud how anyone could doubt the existence of the Creator with masterpieces like trees and flowers as examples of His majestic wonder.

It wasn't long before Joy once again fell into a deep

sleep. A few hours later he woke her and asked, "Who was the first woman to fly around the world?"

"Amelia Earhart," she muttered sleepily.

"What book of the bible follows Genesis?"

She yawned. "Exodus. What happened to my birthday or the president?"

He grinned, knowing she couldn't see him. "These are supposed to be pop quizzes. You had time to think up the answer to those. Go back to sleep. I'll see you in a couple of hours."

"Shouldn't you get some sleep, too?" she asked, her voice muzzy with sleep.

Brian gritted his teeth against the wave of longing and something he refused to name. Reaching for an impersonal tone he said, "My watch has an alarm. I'll sleep. Don't worry about me. I survived my residency just fine. Now, I mean it. Get back to sleep."

After adding more wood to the fire, Brian ducked inside his shelter. And not a moment too soon. The skies opened up as he settled on the ground. He sighed, as the fires started to sputter out. It was going to be a long night.

Three hours later, hoping to avoid going out into the downpour, Brian called out to Joy from his shelter. "What's the capital of New Jersey?"

"Trenton," Joy shouted back. "Now will you go to sleep and leave me alone." There was misery in her every word.

Brian didn't like the way she sounded. So he ducked under one of the extra solar blankets and went over to her shelter. The rain was still coming down, but nowhere near as hard as it had been when it started. "Are you cold? Or wet? Or in pain?"

"No, doctor, I'm tired. And if my partner in this ridiculous misadventure would leave me alone, maybe I could sleep."

"You know, one of the symptoms I'm supposed to look for is irritability. Do you have any idea how hard it is to tell if you're more irritable than usual? You're always in a bad mood."

She sighed. "Brian, please just leave me alone and please don't wake me again. I'd rather die in my sleep than spend another minute awake in this. I don't understand why anyone would go camping and call it a vacation. I really don't. If you wake me again, I swear I'll crawl through the mud and put you out of my misery!"

Without another word Brian left her, hiding a smile. He was sure she was fine. There was no sense in making them both miserable. Or was that more miserable than they already were?

For him it was only Joy's condition and the thought of those kids out there all alone that cast a pall over the night. He closed his eyes and listened to the sound of the rain and the utter quiet surrounding them. For the first time in years Brian felt as if he'd come home. He'd mentioned the cabin his parents had owned to Joy earlier and, in reminding her, he'd reminded himself of those special days long gone.

For him those trips had been less about the companionship of his older brothers, and even his father, and more about time spent in the quiet of the woods. His thinking had always been more focused, his distractions less noticeable, his dreams clearer and his prayers seemed to connect his spirit more completely with the Lord.

Now he once again prayed for guidance and patience with Joy, and that the morning would see her greatly improved. He hated seeing her in pain. He hated seeing her unhappy. Brian knew the plane had meant a great deal to her and was tempted to assume that its loss was partly responsible for her mood. But with the clarity his surroundings brought to him, he knew that, for the most part, it was his own presence that put her in the mood she was in.

He didn't know how he'd fooled himself all these years. He'd thought Joy avoided him because she was uncomfortable in his presence. He'd assumed she no longer resented him for what had happened between them. They'd been young, inexperienced in life and love and had both made mistakes. But now he knew that not only did she still resent him, but he had also held a certain amount of resentment toward her, too. And he'd thought himself above that.

As a pediatric trauma surgeon he was unfortunately kept too busy for anything resembling a life. His incredibly busy career kept life rolling along at nearly the speed of sound. There was little time for introspection about anything but what the next minute, hour or day would bring. The only outside interest he had was stopping at the fitness club on his way home, and he did that so he'd be in the best shape he could be in to increase his stamina in the OR.

Even the faces of the children he was able to save and send home to recover had begun to blur, though those he couldn't save were always with him. He wasn't complaining. His career was rewarding. His days were full of sadness, yes, but there was joy, too.

And there was that word creeping in again. That person.

Joy.

With her so close at hand there seemed no way that he would escape memories of her that night. Memories of what had been. Thoughts of what could have been and never would be. He sighed and rolled over, determined to sleep, and put her where she wanted to be. In his past. But his dreams were of a future he'd long since given up on.

A future with Joy.

Chapter Five

A small scratching sound woke Brian from the mists of a dream. In his present state, caught between fantasy and dawn, he was quietly, completely happy. The rain had long since blown through, leaving behind a crisp breezy day. Sunshine dappled the ground through the shadow of the ever-thickening canopy. Expecting to see Joy outside her shelter, he looked out to find a family of chipmunks scurrying through the campsite, chasing each other. He chuckled at their antics. Then reality crashed down, dispersing the last remnants of the dream.

This was not a family camping trip with Joy and their children sharing their love of nature and each other. He and Joy weren't held together by anything more than the circumstances of a plane crash and six lost children. Banishing the sadness that weighed down his heart, Brian checked on the rations he'd hung from a tree for safekeeping.

He started the fire again and checked on the container he'd set out last night to collect rain water. He was pleased to see that there was enough to fill the water bottles and the canteens he'd found in the emergency packs. After adding purification tablets to the water, Brian crept over to check on Joy.

He was thankful she was sleeping soundly, but dark circles shadowed the delicate skin under her long, curling lashes. It made her appear vulnerable. Weighing their plans against how exhausted she looked, Brian grew troubled with her decision to begin a march to the crash site. She looked fragile, exhausted. How could he even let her try it?

He glanced uphill wondering how long it would take him to get up there to try his cell phone. Staring down at her, Brian made his decision. He scribbled a note and put it with some water and a power bar where she would see it when she woke. After a quick perusal, he grabbed another bar and some water for himself and hurried off to climb the rest of the way up the mountain. With any luck they would be home before nightfall.

Please, let me get back before she wakes up, Lord, he prayed as he glanced back one more time at the almost completely hidden campsite. *Protect her while I'm gone, please.* He winced. *And if You could find a way to keep her asleep while I'm away, I'd sure appreciate it. Otherwise I'm going to have one angry female on my hands when I get back.*

The heavy thud of a chopper flying overhead startled Joy from a sound sleep. She sat up too quickly, forgetting her shoulder and knee. Pain lanced through her body and she moaned. She could have bitten her tongue, expecting Brian to come rushing to her side at any second with his solicitude and practiced bedside manner. But then she realized he was probably too busy waving one of the highly reflective solar blankets at the chopper. More carefully this time, Joy inched forward and pushed back the parachute material that formed the front wall.

Their small, makeshift campsite was utterly deserted.

Full-blown panic blossomed in her heart. Brian was gone. He'd left her. She was alone in the vast Adirondack Forest Preserve in the most dense and dangerous area of the mammoth Forever Wild preserve lands. Only then did she realize how quiet it had suddenly become. The chopper had moved on, never seeing their campsite.

And with it had gone their chance for a quick rescue.

Then Joy glanced back in the shelter and saw a power bar, a bottle of water and a note. She read it aloud. "Joy, I woke with the sun and I decided to chance the hike to the top of this peak. If my cell phone works, they'll be able to find us from the locator chip in my phone and you'll be home before nightfall. I have to try before the phone runs out of power. I should be back before noon if we landed as far up the mountain as I think we did."

"High noon. The perfect time for a showdown," she grumbled. She was furious, afraid and, worst of all, completely powerless.

She couldn't believe he'd do this to her after his show of concern for her injuries. Especially since that annoying concern had included waking her from a sound sleep in the middle of the night to ask his dumb questions. After that she'd lain awake listening to a myriad of scurrying and scratching noises coming from outside the shelter. She'd lain there for hours waiting for something huge to tear apart the flimsy shelter with its razor-sharp teeth and claws in a quest to get to her and make her its next meal.

She'd dozed off only once in the darkness and had awakened abruptly thinking bugs were crawling on her. She'd scrambled to turn on the flashlight Brian had left with her, managing at the last second to stifle a pathetic scream for help. There hadn't been any bugs, of course. Even self-respecting bugs were smart enough not to camp out in the last days of April.

That had done it. Joy had decided to stay awake until she could at least see her hand in front of her face. She'd filled the rest of her night with prayer until the noises faded with dawn's approach. Only then had she felt safe enough to let sleep take her.

Joy inched back into the shelter and wrapped her blanket around her shoulders to ward off the chill in the April air and the feeling of desertion that threatened to crush any reserve of courage. She glanced at her watch for about the hundredth time since making it safely to the ground and began counting the minutes till Brian's promised return. Once again prayer was the only thing that kept her sane, but for the first time in years she was tempted to blubber like a baby.

Last evening, as dusk rolled solidly into night, Brian had sat across the blazing fire waxing poetic about the beauty of the forest and about how he saw God everywhere he looked. As far as Joy was concerned, God had allowed man to invent the internal combustion engine as well as the trains, planes and automobiles it powered so they could look at His Creation from a nice, safe, glass and steel enclosed safety bubble.

She looked around now and could feel nothing of the wide-open spaces, freedom and quiet Brian found there. Instead she felt claustrophobic. As if the trees and animals were reaching out to get her. And far from quiet! How could anyone call the constant chatter of the birds anything but irritatingly noisy?

Joy was a city girl who had only just learned to appreciate the Chester County burbs. She'd never learned to be comfortable in the dense forests she skimmed over almost daily. Maybe all the rescues she helped with and all the smoke jumpers she'd flown into the dangers inherent in forest fires had compounded her childhood terror. Whatever the reason, she just couldn't seem to conquer her fears. And she felt absolutely ridiculous about it.

The only good thing happening in this situation was that, so far, she seemed to be able to hide it all from Brian. Because one thing she knew she couldn't tolerate was him laughing at her and gloating and poking at her armor because he'd found a chink in it. It was bad enough he knew how much more experienced and competent he was in the wilderness.

Looking around the little campsite Brian had set up, Joy had to admit he was both competent and experienced. She also had to admit being there with Brian was better than being there alone.

He'd surprised her with his knowledge, but more with his strength, agility and resourcefulness. Now that she thought about it, smart people were often resource-ful people. And he was certainly not the tenderfooted bookworm she'd always thought. He hadn't needed her advice to scale the tree she'd been caught in anymore than she'd need his advice on flying.

His strong and toned body, though, still shocked and bothered her on an elemental level she refused to ex-amine. Which made it more imperative that she hide her fear and get him to understand that, though he knew how to survive, she knew how to get them rescued. Be-cause keeping him at arm's length and subordinate to her was suddenly as important to her as survival.

Brian fought a growing sense of unease as he climbed higher and higher. He didn't think it had any-thing to do with the helicopter he'd failed to flag down. Oak, maple and beech had quickly given way to birch after the rescue chopper passed him by. Now, as the way grew steeper there were more and more conifers. Fi-nally, still plagued by vague disquiet, he forced himself to try analyzing the source of his worry.

Joy.

Something about the way she'd been acting didn't add up. Though she'd worked hard to hide it, she was anxious in a way he had never seen her. It was a trait to worry about in someone who was usually as self-assured as she was. In fact, the only story he'd ever heard from her brother Jim that painted Joy as being less than fear-less was from a period of time when she was about eight.

The Lovell's had rented a movie for Christmas night—*The Wizard of Oz*. And for weeks after Joy had plagued the household with sleepless nights due to nightmares the movie caused her to have. If he remembered correctly, Dorothy's forest trek and the flying monkeys had scared young Joy, and not the wicked witch.

At the time, Brian had thought it quite hilarious to chant, "Lions and tigers and bears," when she was least suspecting it. He'd reveled in the new information he'd gained to torture her.

Could it be possible? Could dragon-slaying Joy be afraid of the beautiful woodlands surrounding them? If that was true, he'd left her to battle her fear alone. His hand went automatically to his chest. The thought caused him to ache. He'd been hoping to save her from a long hike to the plane. But maybe he shouldn't left her after all.

Was she hiding her fear out of pride? Did she think he would tease her? Still try to torture her the way he had back then? Joy had always been such a puzzle to him. Now he had to wonder if she'd been reluctant to abandon her plane because she'd preferred the risk of a crash landing to a long hike back to civilization?

Unsettled now, Brian took out his cell phone. He'd entered the high country and still his cell phone had no service. Suddenly he couldn't stand the idea of Joy waking alone and frightened. And it looked as if he was on a fool's errand anyway. Without another thought, he did an about-face and started back down the mountain.

Joy sat near the fire, her makeshift crutch next to her. She looked at it and looked around the little campsite then she eyed the crutch again. What was this? The

Swiss Family Robinson? Was there nothing the man couldn't improvise?

A squawk from above made her blood run cold, reminding her of another thing besides inconveniences the Swiss family had been forced to contend with. She expected some wild creature to come bursting out of the bushes with hunger in its beady little eyes and an image of her on its dinner plate. She eyed a blue jay that squawked at her from a low branch with suspicion. She expected an angry flock of the feathered creatures to start dive-bombing her at her any moment.

But then a new sound joined the din from the birds. It was a cracking, rustling noise she hadn't heard until then. Her heart sped up and she knew what real terror felt like. It was nowhere near noon so it couldn't be Brian returning. If it wasn't him, she knew from all the noise that it had to be something really big.

And it continued to move ever closer.

Joy struggled to her feet and held the crutch like a weapon. Heart pounding, she stood waiting for death in the jaws of a bear or something even bigger. Something the pitiful weapon in her hands wasn't going to have the slightest effect on.

That was how Brian found her, blast him!

He pushed through the brush surrounding the campsite and stepped into the small clearing. Relieved and furious, she glared at him, fighting the temptation to take a swing at him any way for scaring a year off her life.

For leaving her.

"Uh-oh. I'd hoped you might sleep till I got back," he admitted.

She nonchalantly lowered the crutch and balanced on it, trying to act as if she'd just been in the process of swinging it into position. "Did you? Did you also hear the chopper that passed directly overhead? It was gone by the time I could get out of the shelter."

"Yeah, I tried to get their attention from where I was but the trees must have been too thick. And I realized as I was coming down from above why they probably didn't see the camp. Out in the open a solar blanket would reflect the sun back up at them and act like a signal mirror to catch their attention. In here, all the foil did was reflect the trees. Unfortunately it was perfect camouflage. I hardly saw our camp till I was right on top of it. I'm sorry. I was only trying to keep us dry last night."

Joy might be angry about his solo trek but she couldn't blame him for making the night much more comfortable than it would have been without the rain protection.

"You did your best," was all she could say without diminishing her righteous anger.

"But it kills me to think those kids felt what we just did when the chopper didn't see us. That they might have seen us when we flew overhead yesterday and I didn't see them."

She felt her anger surge again. "And had you been here when the chopper flew by, you might have figured this out and we might be our way home right now. But no, you had to go off tilting at windmills."

Brian frowned. "How do you know I didn't get through to anyone?"

"Because the chances of your cell phone working here are slim to none. Why do you think I carry a satellite phone? I don't care what the commercials say. You don't always get reception from isolated areas. The nearest cell tower is probably fifty miles from here if not farther."

"Why didn't you say that yesterday?"

"Because we got off the subject of the cell phone and my brains were a little scrambled. Besides that, I thought we'd settled this. I'd already won the argument. Why would I waste my breath with unnecessary explanations? Look, Brian, I'm willing to admit that you know what you're about out here. I'll bow to your expertise about our health, but you have to stop going off half cocked where getting rescued is concerned. You said you understood about getting to the plane," she countered.

Brian winced slightly. "And I do." He paused and his eyes seemed to cloud over as if he'd drifted far away. Then his gaze cleared and he stared at her for long moment and said, "For what it's worth, I'm sorry I struck out on my own. But you have to admit you weren't up to starting out at dawn. In fact, I'm not sure you're up to it now."

She was so tempted to agree that she held her breath to keep from betraying her level of discomfort. One benefit of his solo trek was that it would be a shorter day hiking. "I told you I'll make it. And I will," she said after a pause then she shifted her stance a little. "We've wasted enough time today. How do you think we should go about carrying all this?"

"One of the things I did while you were sleeping yesterday was to rig up a backpack for myself out of a parachute harness. I hated to waste the suture kits to stitch it, but we may need these supplies."

"You can't carry it all."

Brian stared at her for long moment then winked. "Watch me, sweetheart," he quipped and turned away to begin packing up and breaking down the shelters. "It should take me half an hour. In the meantime, you should rest. I'll give you that painkiller I promised now. By the time we're ready to move out, it should kick in."

Joy fervently hoped that it would.

Brian glanced behind him to check on Joy. He leaned back against a rock and waited for her to catch up. She was a trooper he had to give her that, but her labored pace was painful to watch even though his idea for the crutch seemed to work well. Back at the campsite her anger had nearly convinced him he'd been wrong about the possibility that she was afraid. She'd looked like a proud, strong Valkyrie standing there wielding that crutch. But then he had to wonder what she'd thought she would need to fight off—a two-or four-legged menace?

Then, as often happened to him, his mother's voice echoed from the recesses of his mind. Around the time Joy was fourteen he'd been teasing her. Not that there was anything different about that, but this time Thomasina Peterson had come down on him like a ton of bricks for hurting Joy's feelings.

Indignant, Brian had countered that Joy gave as good as she got. She wasn't hurt, just angry, he'd said. His mother's kind face had creased just a little more with a sad smile. No, she'd explained, Joy was the kind of person who hid her hurt behind anger. She'd explained the difference between his home and Joy's—that there was no place in the Lovell household for hurt feminine feelings. Basically, she said Joy had been taught from an early age to process hurt and make it anger. She'd even wondered aloud if Jimmy Lovell knew his youngest was a girl. She'd gone on to add that Joy was very nearly a young lady and that as a young man it was his duty to protect young women, not torture them.

Brian had gone off to sulk, annoyed that his mom would try to wreck the one bit of fun he'd had in his life at the time—a sad testament to his teenage years in the blue-collar neighborhood. Being top in your class didn't earn you street credibility, that was for sure.

After that, teasing her had lost its luster and he'd tried to be nice to her. She'd responded in kind and they'd struck up a wary friendship. A few more years passed and he came to be grateful. He'd had considerably less to apologize for when he'd come home from college for winter break and saw that the cygnet had become a swan in his absence. He'd wanted to date her then, but he'd waited till she was in her senior year of high school. And then it had only taken months for his dreams to turn to dust.

Brian dragged his thoughts back to the present and focused on Joy as she limped toward him. Thus far she'd refused his help, but he could see she was tiring quickly. "Suppose you rest here for a little while. I'd like to scout that area off to the left," he said and pointed to a small sunlit meadow on a parallel course to theirs. "This trail's getting rocky and pretty steep. I thought maybe there might be an easier path leading down the mountain beyond that meadow."

Joy nodded and Brian took off his pack. He untied the gurney pad and tossed it down for her to sit on. The vinyl-covered pad made the pack bulkier than he would've liked and at first he'd intended to leave it behind. It had already served its purpose of cushioning the bundle he'd dragged with him out of the plane. But leaving it had bothered him. His father had taught him and his brothers not to leave a mark on the wilderness with discarded things. Then, as if to cement his instincts, Joy had insisted she would carry it if necessary. Taking that as a sign that she was a lot more uncomfortable than she was willing to let on, he'd decided to bring it along. So he'd rearranged things and they'd gotten started for the plane.

As he tramped toward the meadow, Brian remembered their short exchange earlier in the day. His mother had been both right and wrong. Joy did hide hurt with anger, but she had never wanted or needed his protection within a relationship between them. He was beginning to think what she'd needed was for him to show he had confidence in her abilities. If that was the case, then he'd failed her.

Maybe that was why since Joy, he only dated petite brunettes—women as different from Joy as he could find. The thought gave him pause. So why, if they were her polar opposite, did those women always lose their fascination for him so quickly? None of them made his heart pound. His head spin. Or his heart ache with tenderness and admiration. And those were all the things he felt now as he watched Joy fight pain and fatigue with steadfast determination and courage.

No wonder just glancing at her across a room bothered him so deeply. He was tired of the animosity—he missed her friendship and he'd never been so attracted to any of his petite brunettes. Though they could never be more to each other than friends, it would be nice if they could at least have that again. He sighed. They could have been so happy if he had been what she'd needed and if she could have been what he wanted.

Brian was shocked to realize that he desperately wanted to be what Joy needed right now. Remembering the tired look on her face as she settled onto the mat, he wondered if that were possible, considering their history. He was nearly sure he couldn't get her to rest for long, but at least he could find an easier route to the valley.

Rolling his sore shoulders and shaking a cramp out of one of his arms, Brian moved swiftly across the meadow. The pack he'd left with Joy was heavy and he was out of practice with this kind of exercise. He made himself promise—when they got back home, he'd begin taking more time for relaxation, for life.

Nearly at the far edge of the meadow, he'd just spotted a deer path when he heard Joy's terrified scream. It had taken a full five minutes to get as far as he was, but Brian made it back in two minutes flat. He didn't know what he expected to find but it wasn't Joy cowering against the rock he used for a seat a short while ago. Or the adorable bear cub, sitting back on its haunches, sniffing the air then licking its paws. He was so relieved that she wasn't in immediate danger, he chuckled.

"It isn't funny," Joy snapped.

He looked around, realizing she was right. It was easy to see why people got themselves into trouble with bears. "No. He's cute but you're right. It really isn't funny. I'm guessing you didn't see the mother."

"No, thank the Lord. I woke up and it was standing over me making weird noises. Then he licked me." She shuddered and wiped her cheek. "It startled me, is all."

"No doubt," Brian said, reaching for a neutral tone and schooling his lips in a straight line. A grin at that moment could be disaster. She was so prickly anything could start another argument and they really didn't have time for one. He decided not to mention the fact that she'd been wide-awake and trying to press her back through solid rock, looking more scared to death than startled when he arrived. It seemed as if his mother had taught him something after all.

When to shut his mouth.

"Come on. We have to get out of here," he urged and offered her his hand.

"Then it is dangerous?" she asked and put her hand in his.

He pulled her to her feet and helped her lean against the rock. After bending down to pick up the crutch and pad she'd been sitting on, he explained. "The cub isn't too much of a danger on its own, but its mother will be if we're between her and her baby or she doesn't like how close we are. Since we don't know where she is, we'd better be on our way."

Brian didn't hand her her crutch, but stepped to her left side after shouldering the pack and tucking the gurney pad under his arm. "I know you don't want my help but we'll get away from here faster if you accept it. I think I found a deer path at the other side of the meadow. That will be a little easier going than this trail. It looks like our best bet from here."

Prepared for her to fight his help, he was surprised when she only nodded and wrapped her arm around his waist. He did the same to her and wished it didn't feel so right to have her by his side.

Chapter Six

Almost in a daze, Joy gave in and let Brian help her. He led them back the way he'd come and out into the meadow. The bright sunshine warmed her skin. Minutes later though, she swallowed deeply as they approached the tree line, fighting an instinctive fear and a corresponding tightening of her muscles. Not long after their return to the darkness of the dense forest, they came to a stream and were able to replenish their dwindling water supply.

As Brian had hoped, the deer track was easier to navigate. Because of that they were able to cover more territory than if she'd gone it alone. But, though his assistance helped her toward their goal and lessened the pain in her knee and ankle, his nearness was sheer mental torture.

As they trudged along in silence, Joy found herself going over the last twenty-four hours. She realized they had been all her worst nightmares come true.

First had come the rude awakening that her passenger was the one person she least wanted to spend time with. Then the inevitability of the crash of her plane had forced her to parachute with him into one of the wildest parts of the northeast. Next she'd awakened to find herself hurt, out of her element and completely dependent on the man whose rejection had broken her eighteen-year-old heart twelve years ago.

It wasn't bad enough that she'd had to deal with a long, torturous night in a crude shelter. Oh, no. Following a night spent huddled in the dark, quaking with fear, she'd experienced a truly terrifying moment when she woke. Alone in the makeshift camp with miles and miles of wilderness between herself and civilization, she'd thought nothing could be worse.

She'd been wrong. Because none of the rest of it compared to waking from a short, accidental rest on the trail staring into the furry face of the most horrendous death she could ever have imagined. She shuddered at the memory.

Joy could still hear Brian's chuckle after he'd burst upon the scene that she'd found anything but funny. He'd once tormented her from behind doors and garden walls and trash cans in the back alley for an entire summer with the chant of "Lions and tigers and bears." The memory had echoed from the recesses of her mind and she'd been all set to lash out at him. Instead he'd helped her up, confirmed the bear cub as a possible danger, then whisked her away to safer territory.

Brian's reaction left her off balance and forced her to reevaluate everything she'd thought about him in the twelve years since they broke up. It didn't take long to face the difficult truth. She'd been wrong about Brian for years. She didn't know how she'd managed to convince herself that he was nothing more than an older version of the boy who'd tormented her half her life. But she had.

She'd fallen in love with him before he'd even called a moratorium on that sort of behavior so she didn't know how she could have been so blind. Blinking back tears that had little to do with her injuries, she stumbled to a stop and Brian reacted immediately.

"Too fast?" he asked, clearly concerned.

She shook her head. "I think I should try it alone for a while. This is…um…putting too much of a strain everywhere else."

Brian frowned, but nodded and handed her the crutch he'd so carefully constructed. "Just let me know if you need to stop, or go slower or if you need help," he said and started forward alone, taking the lead, testing the footing on the trail. His strong back, his slightly too-long hair curling at his hairline, the way he moved along the path, snared her attention. Joy couldn't seem to take her eyes off him. She stood watching as he moved away from her with sure-footed ease until she could see only the top of his head. With a sigh, she followed.

Brian stopped once in a while to help her negotiate a difficult stretch of the trail, then let go without a word and started off alone again. After enduring the neutral look in his eyes for half the day, Joy came to understand the real source of her misery today where Brian was concerned. He'd been decent and solicitous, but he would do the same for any stranger. In fact, while practically glued to her side, he'd treated her exactly as if she *were* a stranger. It was as if that whirlwind courtship had never happened. They were now, at best, childhood adversaries who'd become a couple for a brief moment in time before going their separate ways.

And that was the crux of the problem. Each act of kindness reminded her of all that might have been. The loneliness she battled each day was worse now because he was so near, yet so far. When he'd loved her, he'd done it in all the wrong ways but, at that moment, it didn't seem to matter. Because if he was still the man she'd once thought him to be, then she'd lost him for the reason she'd always feared.

She hadn't been enough.

He'd been wrong to demand she become someone she wasn't and that usually made her angry. Today it only made her sad.

Joy limped along determined to keep up. She wanted to get this forced togetherness over with as soon as possible. She carefully watched where she put her feet. Mooning over what might have been was futile and self-destructive, she lectured herself. What was important today was survival and continuing on. If she fell, they would probably have to stop for the day, so she was cautious and deliberate with her every step.

Fighting a wave of exhaustion, Joy intentionally turned her mind to other matters. When she did, she felt an intense shame strike deep within her. Not once since waking, trapped and tangled in a tree with Brian for a rescuer, had she considered the reason they'd been out there in the first place. In her anger at Brian when he returned to camp, she hadn't even noticed when he'd mentioned them. The children.

If she was afraid, how much more terrified were they?

All she'd been thinking about was herself—*her* fear, *her* discomfort, *her* pain. She'd wallowed in self-pity and anger at Brian, never once examining the rest of the consequences of her failure as a searcher. She'd crashed and those children were still out there somewhere alone, maybe hurt and almost definitely afraid. Suddenly sick with guilt, Joy pushed ahead more determined than ever to keep up.

They'd hiked about a mile more when Brian stopped at a fork in the trail. He bent at the hips and braced his hands on his knees. Then he just stood there staring at the ground for a long moment.

"Brian? Is something wrong?" she asked, gaining on him.

He hunkered down as if to get a closer look at whatever had grabbed his attention. "Tracks," he said, absently looking from right to left.

"Who are you all of a sudden? Daniel Boone?" she quipped. Stepping to the side, Joy saw what he did. There were several sets of footprints. "Oh. I see what you mean. They sure are footprints, aren't they? You think they're from the lost kids or a search party?"

Brian stood and placed his foot next to one of the prints. All the prints were much smaller. "Not adults. That's for sure. It has to be those kids. I'm no expert but these prints were made when this was all mud through here. They could have been made after one of the storms last week, I suppose." He paused. "Still, I'd think the deer that travel through here would have obliterated some of this by now if these were made that long ago. I'm thinking they were made after yesterday's storm."

Joy had a good sense of direction even if she couldn't see the merits of the forest while surrounded by its trees. "That puts them in this area but it means they're headed away from the plane. I'm sure it went down off in that direction," she said, pointing to the right.

Brian turned to face her and Joy looked up into his dark brown eyes. She was surprised to read indecision and reluctance in his gaze for the first time. It was oddly disconcerting. He was always so sure of himself. There'd been a time when she'd have reveled in his hesitation. She'd always found his self-confidence annoying, but right then, she needed him secure in his decisions. "What? What is it?" she asked.

"I'm not sure what to do," he replied, confirming her worst fears. "Do we go after them? Or do I get you to that plane as quickly as possible so you can check out that transponder? You can't go traipsing all over the preserve in the condition you're in. But even though we know there are search parties looking for all of us, those kids have been alone out here for too long already."

She wanted to get to the plane but she knew that if those kids were half as afraid as she was, they needed Brian, too. He might not be able to effect a rescue but he could keep them safe until one came along. Besides, after they found the children, they could all make their way to the plane together. She started off down the footprint-marked trail.

"Whoa. Where are you going?" Brian demanded.

She looked back and raised an eyebrow. "After those kids. What did you think?"

"I thought something more along the lines of you staying here tucked in a shelter where you could rest while I take off after them."

The man was impossible! She battled down fresh, utter panic at once again hearing him toy with the idea of leaving her behind. "I thought we had this discussion yesterday and again this morning. We don't separate the downed party. It isn't as if the footprints aren't headed downhill. It's the right general direction. We can always double back toward the plane once we find the kids in the valley. What were you planning to do? Make them trudge back up here just to get me?"

Brian had to admit she was right. After nearly a week wandering alone in the forest he doubted those kids would have any strength to spare for an unnecessary side trip. Still, Brian was uneasy about her continuing on. He could see the pain in her eyes, and they were beginning to glaze with the fever she was trying to hide. He'd given her a loaded dose of penicillin that morning hoping this wouldn't happen but, like everything else on this ill-fated journey, that seemed to be going wrong, too. She was clearly developing an infection.

"Are you sure you won't wait here?" he asked. "Don't try to tell me you aren't in agony."

She grinned and tilted her head. "That's funny, I thought I was in New York. Now let's get this show on the road."

He chuckled at her Uncle George's patented corny

joke then sobered. Why couldn't she just do things the easy way? "Joy, I'm serious. I'd hate to see you do permanent damage. You need rest and you're not looking too good."

"If one of those kids dies, it'll be a lot more serious than me developing a permanent limp."

Well, he couldn't argue with that logic. So he nodded and once again took the lead on the trail. But he wasn't happy about the situation. He also knew she needed something to distract her so she could get her mind off her pain.

"I heard you bought a house," he said, hoping the opening gambit would get her talking. Women loved talking about their homes. And though she seemed to deny her femininity, she was unmistakably a woman after all.

"It's a carriage house actually," she explained. "I fell in love with it the minute I saw it. It was one of those things that happens and you just know the Lord had His hand in it."

"Like how?" he asked. He'd probably heard the story from his mom but he wouldn't have wanted to hear about a house he hadn't bought for her. He'd probably put it out of his mind as soon as he could. Just as he knew she'd accepted the Lord a few years ago but didn't remember exactly when or how it had come about. He remembered thinking he was glad, but he'd felt guilty that he hadn't even bothered presenting the Gospel to her when he'd had the chance. It seemed he had failed her in every way he could.

"…and that's when I met Adam Boyer," she was

saying when he realized she'd begun to answer his question about her house. "Who would ever think I'd meet a guy who owns an estate at one of my brother's barbeques? Anyway, the carriage house sits on the front corner of Adam's property. He mentioned that he'd decided to sell it and a little of the land surrounding it. It sounded perfect and it is." She laughed.

He'd bet it was the first time he heard her laugh in years. There was nothing quite like seeing Joy happy. He didn't have to look back to know how her blue eyes sparkled and what that smile that could light a dark room looked like. It had been hiding in his memory for years.

"So what's the place look like?" he asked, surprised to find he really wanted to know.

Once again, she laughed. "Like the seven dwarfs are going to walk out the front door at any moment."

"Dwarfs?" Joy was every bit of six foot tall. It didn't sound like the perfect house for her. "Do you have to duck to get in and out the doors?"

"No. The doors are the regular size. It's just that the house looks sort of like it came straight out of a fairy tale. A hedge of tall boxwood hides it from the road and drive and it's partially covered in ivy. It has two arch-top carriage doors on the ground floor and a front door that matches them. All the windows arch, too, and they're made of diamond-patterned, leaded glass. Like I said. It's a fairy tale come to life in wood, stone and mortar."

Before this he would have guessed Joy would rather have a furnished airplane hangar than a storybook house. "So is it convenient to your airfield?" he asked, instead of voicing his clearly faulty conclusion. His perceptions of her were changing so rapidly he couldn't seem to switch tracks fast enough. For years, hearing about her adventures, he'd come to think he'd had a lucky escape. He'd once joked to his older brother that she was nothing but a guy with female equipment. He was beginning to see why Greg had looked at him as if he'd lost his mind.

She didn't answer his question about her commute for a while but just kept plodding along behind him. Finally, after a long pause, she said, "It's about ten miles from the field but it's not a bad ride because they're back roads. Sometimes, though, I wish I could just fly there and back. But I don't think my neighbors would appreciate my parking the Huey in my backyard and scaring their horses."

Brian chuckled. "I always did see you as a city girl. I was surprised when you moved out to Chester County."

"I *am* a city girl. I moved from Riverside to Wilmington, Delaware, to be close to Agape Air and I lived happily there for years, but I wanted to be closer to Mom and my brother, especially since Jim married Crystal and they gave me a niece."

"Yeah, I enjoy Greg's tribe, too."

"I hope so, since you work with kids. I assume you must like them."

For the first time all day Brian felt the knot appear in his stomach that he'd come to associate with work. "Liking kids sometimes makes my job harder. A lot of the time they're unconscious and in critical condition when I first see them. At best they're scared half to death and in pain. It's hard seeing them that way. Especially since most of them don't understand what's happened to them and they have no say in what the adults around them have decided to do. I don't usually have the time to explain any of it to the actual patient so a lot of them see me as the enemy."

"Still it must be satisfying or you wouldn't work so hard."

He sighed unconsciously. "Sometimes I think working hard is just a habit with me. Don't get me wrong, it's very satisfying to see a child go home to a bright future because I used the skill God gave me. But sometimes it's a little scary, too. You see that innocent face and know his or her life is in your hands. And you know the clock is ticking. I'm sure you know from the rescue work you've done that there really is a critical hour in trauma cases. A lot of that time is gone before I ever see the victim. There have been days recently when I've wondered why I put myself in that position day in and day out."

Brian glance back to gauge her progress. She moved with a fluid grace even though not with her usual confident near-swagger. "At times like this do you question your career?" he asked. What she did and why she did it were a huge mystery to him.

She hesitated, then shook her head. "I enjoy flying— yesterday's mishap notwithstanding," she added with a grimace. "The only time I get stressed is when I'm trying to balance the bank accounts."

"I heard you're buying old George out," he commented then started forward again. "I guess you got what you wanted."

"For the most part," she answered.

It was an ambiguous reply, at best. Brian found himself saying, "I know it's a hard life. I hope you're happy." And surprised as he was to have said it, he really did hope she'd found what she wanted in life. He was proud of what she'd accomplished, though he was sure she cared little for his opinion. What did he have to be proud of where she was concerned anyway? The only thing he'd ever done was try to get in the way of what she wanted to do with her life. He was beginning to think he'd been dead wrong and not merely clumsy in his attempt to save her from a lifetime of hard work and danger.

Having run out of topics to introduce, Brian fell into silence as they continued to descend the deer track toward the valley. Joy didn't initiate any conversation, either. The terrain began to flatten out and he heard Joy quietly call his name. He turned and went back to her side.

In her hands she held a stuffed bear that must have slipped his notice. She handed it to him. "It can't be one of theirs. I got the impression they were all junior-high-age kids. Maybe my brother was unusual but I can't imagine Jim taking a stuffed bear on a hike with six other kids at that age."

"Take my word for it, it wouldn't have made a guy real popular even back then. Still, even though it's damp and dirty, I don't think this bear has been out here all winter. And this isn't an area I would expect anyone to bring a young child, especially this early in the year."

"I'm trying to remember what Russ Dempsey said about them. He said they'd rescued one of the boys and his pastor and that the pastor had been leading the kids and that they'd gotten lost."

"And he said all of them were under thirteen," Brian put in. "Come to think of it, I don't think I heard Mr. Dempsey say how young the youngest boy is." He raked his fingers through his hair and looked at the bear. "We have to find those kids but you can't go on much longer today. When we get to the valley, I'll set up the shelters again and get a fire going. After that, while it's still light, I'll try to look for them. They can't be very far ahead of us."

Joy's eyes widened like a deer caught in a powerful pair of headlights. She stared at him as if trying to gauge his thoughts. Again he wondered if she'd ever gotten over her fear of the wilderness. There was no sense asking, though. If she thought he saw a vulnerability in her, she'd dig her heels in twice as hard to hide it. He also didn't want to chance putting an end to what had become an undeclared truce between them and that would be sure to do it.

Instead he went on trying to reassure her without seeming to. "I probably won't be much farther away than shouting distance and I won't be gone past dark because it's too dangerous tromping around unfamiliar territory at night."

"I pray you find them before dark."

She looked down at the bedraggled teddy bear he still

held and did just that. Joy prayed aloud for the un-known children but she never mentioned herself when he knew she was in severe pain. She was quite a woman. Too bad he was only now beginning to realize it—twelve years too late.

"They must be so afraid," she whispered, looking back up at Brian. The worried look in her eyes would be enough to melt the hardest heart.

"My worry isn't so much that they're afraid, Joy. The security of home and maybe some counseling should take care of that. It's the possibility of exposure, dehy-dration and starvation that have me worried. Those are real life and death issues," he explained, but Joy still looked unsure and, he realized, guilty, too.

He wanted to reassure her that the crash hadn't been her fault, but Brian knew he was the last person she would accept or want comfort from. He hadn't bought her excuse earlier that his help was causing her pain. She just hadn't been able to stand being near him no matter how much his help lessened her pain. He'd had no idea he'd hurt her this badly or that she hated him this much.

Remembering the bear she'd kept hidden in her room as a child, he handed her back the bear she'd found. Maybe she could draw a little comfort from the child's toy. "Here, you take care of old Humphrey."

She took it and smiled, falling back into an old game. "Humphrey?"

Brian grinned. "Wasn't that your bear's name?" He knew it wasn't but when they were sparring, she didn't look so sad.

Joy arched an eyebrow and eyed him with pretend annoyance. "Actually *her* name was Josephine. I think *this* bear looks more like a Mildred," she said with a cheeky grin of her own then looked down at the bear. "Honestly, Mildred, men just have no clue. Do they?"

There, he thought as he stifled a laugh. That was much better. She was his Joy again. Brian's smile faded as he watched her struggle ahead. She'd never be his again. She was the wrong woman for him and he'd seen that clearly twelve years ago. Why was he now beginning to fear that he'd rejected a diamond in the rough as flawed, foolishly missing the very features that made her priceless?

Chapter Seven

Joy reached out to accept Brian's hand once again when they came to an extremely steep section of the deer path they'd been following. She steadfastly ignored the tingle that shot up her arm at his touch as he helped her down that last steep embankment before they reached the floor of the valley. Resolutely, she took her hand back and held it out for the crutch.

Digging deep for composure, Joy lectured herself not to be stupid enough to still be attracted to Brian Peterson after all the hurt he'd caused her. She couldn't be attracted to him. She just wouldn't be.

That settled in her mind, if not her heart, Joy walked along next to him trying to banish her awareness of him by turning her attention to the valley ahead. Verdant meadows stretched out before them. A wide stream shimmered in the distance as it flowed along at a quick pace. A pink-orange sunset cast an odd light on the valley.

She stopped and looked back at where they'd been

and noticed how the odd sunset lent a rosy color to the steep rock walls that ran the length of the valley on their side of the wide stream. Brian's decision to follow the deer path had been prudent, and not just because they had stumbled upon the children's trail. The deer path seemed to be the only trail on this side of the mountain that led into the valley that didn't included a steep descent down what looked to be a hundred-foot rock wall.

With her shoulder aching, her arm on fire and her knee and ankle not far from agonizing and useless, Joy would never have been able traverse those cliffs, even with Brian's help.

"I wonder how much more beautiful the Garden of Eden was if just a little corner of the world can look like this," Brian wondered aloud, his quiet reverent tone drawing her attention back to him.

Annoyed at this new penchant of hers for admiring even the tone of his voice, she replied, "You really are depressingly provincial, you know. You spend more time waxing poetic about the great outdoors than Teddy Roosevelt did. The Sierra Club should hire you as a spokesman."

Brian didn't bristle, but grinned. "Blame that on my father and those weekends in the mountains." He sighed in a way that sounded like relief. "I missed this more than I'd realized. Too bad it took a plane crash to get me to slow down enough to smell the roses again. I know it might sound foolish to you, and I'm sorry you lost your plane and that you got hurt, but I'm not sorry this happened. I guess the Lord was trying to get my attention and I wouldn't listen."

"Well, I wish I hadn't gotten caught up in your rustic rejuvenation," she told him, but the casual way he spoke of the Lord's influence on his life struck her.

Considering who his parents were, the depth of Brian's faith shouldn't surprise her, but it did. Maybe because Brian had never been one to talk about his faith even though his parents and brother had.

Now that she looked back on it, the friendship between the older Petersons and Lovells seemed even odder now than it had back then. That there was an unmistakable difference between the two families was something that had always been glaringly obvious.

Bud Peterson was a plumber who'd made enough money that he could have moved his family to the suburbs. But his business was in Riverside so he'd stayed, living and working among his neighbors. Her father was a cop and no one made enough money to live comfortably serving the public of Riverside. The only thing that kept the two families on a somewhat even financial footing was that the Petersons didn't spend anywhere near the level they could have and Joy's mother had her own career.

Although many wouldn't call hairdressing a career, it was something her mother still loved doing and it supported her nicely now. She owned the salon that she'd opened with Jimmy Lovell's life insurance in the little town center of Village Green, Pennsylvania. She lived upstairs from the shop not far from Jim and Crystal's house, or Joy's, and still looked forward every day to doing her job.

The difference between the families was more than

financial, though. Her father had been a tough, fair man who'd worked hard but he'd played even harder. Beer, sports and cars were his interests outside work. It was in sports, cars and love of their families where he had found a common ground with the gentle, soft-spoken Bud Peterson.

Her father had taken the name of the Lord in vain on an hourly basis, but never around Bud. She remembered Jim once saying that if it hadn't been for the Petersons, the name of Jesus would have been nothing but a swear word to him. The couple had lived their faith and let their lives and the way they lived them speak of the Lord. It had eventually spoken to both Jim and Joy.

Though she had been young at the time, Joy remembered the grace with which the couple had endured the death of their middle son, Tommy, to a drug overdose. And she remembered her gruff take-no-prisoners father, hugging his friend and assuring him that he hadn't been at fault.

It had been Bud Peterson her father asked for when he lay dying of an assailant's bullet. Why Bud had been able to lead Jimmy Lovell to the Lord when his son and daughter and Bud's oldest son, who was a minister, had failed was one of those things that would remain a mystery into eternity. The most important thing was that it had happened.

"Does that stream help you at all to pinpoint where we are?" Brian asked, yanking her back to the present.

She blinked and focused again on the valley and on the wide, gurgling stream that rushed through the center of it. "It looks as if it may have flooded its banks.

That changes the look of it. But even if it maintained its usual course there are several valleys like this in the Adirondacks and I only know how they look from the air."

Knowing how important getting their bearing was and not wanting to give up, she glanced around and limped forward. She closed her eyes trying to visualize where they'd been when the weather had turned ugly in an instant of lightning and blinding rain. But the wind had buffeted their small aircraft and she'd been too busy trying to keep them aloft to take notice of their course. It didn't take long in an aircraft to lose track of how many mountains you traversed when you couldn't see past the windshield. And, of course, it didn't help that she'd lost the map when she'd jumped.

They stood on the floor of the valley with mountains rising all around them. The mountain directly across the valley rose from the valley floor in a sheer rocky cliff. The mountain they'd just come down did as well, with the exception of the terrain around Brian's deer path. Two mountains rose more gently to the east and one to the west. Until that moment she'd had no idea of the monumental task that lay before them. Between them and the plane stood miles and miles of rough danger-ous terrain that from their current vantage point, looked almost straight up.

She felt her scalp prickle and her blood run cold. Joy frowned and fought off a wave of fear. She just might know about where they were and why they hadn't heard or seen any more search planes. The tumultuous wind of the freak storm had blown them into the more remote and little-used area of the preserve. The search had not been centered on this group of mountains and valleys at all.

If the transponder wasn't working and if her radio messages hadn't gone out, they were on their own. The lack of search plans more or less confirmed those fears. There was no way to know how far off course they'd been blown. One look at Brian's expression told her he suspected there was no rescue on the way.

"I'm not sure. It all looks so different from down here," she hastened to say. She didn't know if she was trying to reassure herself or Brian. Maybe both. Maybe neither. "I'm not sure of anything but that the plane's up there," she said, pointing to the tallest, most-distant peak of the valley. "And without knowing which way the nearest town is or how far it is, that transponder and the plane's radio are our best hope for a rescue that I can think of." She sighed. "But it went in pretty far up there."

They stared at each other. As if by some silent communication, Brian put his hand on her shoulder and nodded, letting her know that he understood the harsh reality of the situation. "It won't seem so far away after a good night's sleep. And speaking of sleep, I'd better get going on the shelters. Maybe we should move in closer to that stream, though. Can you make it a little farther?"

She nodded. "I've been thinking about the kids," Joy said. "If you can, maybe you should make one of the shelters big enough for you and them. We may have them with us by tonight if those were their tracks we saw."

Brian nodded, looking worried as they started a slow progress across the valley floor. Considering those lost kids, Joy knew what had to be done. She gripped her crutch tightly. It was the most difficult thing she'd needed to say since they'd parted twelve years earlier when she'd wished him a good life and walked away without meaning a word of it.

This time she meant what she said but it was harder to put voice to it. However much they'd avoided saying so, they both knew there were no planes looking for them where they were. It would mean hours alone for her, but the kids were just as alone and a lot more helpless than she was.

"Um…Bri, if we don't find them today, we really should stay here while you search for them using this as a base camp. You said you don't think they could be far ahead of us."

As if on cue, they heard a pain-filled scream from the direction of the stream. Joy nearly jumped out of her skin. Brian took off like a shot in that direction. Unwilling to await his return and concerned for the children, Joy followed as quickly as her aching leg would allow.

When she arrived she found Brian kneeling over the prone body of a boy. He lay at the base of a pile of boulders near the swollen stream. Five other dirty, disheveled boys stood around looking frightened and worried, staring at the boy on the ground. Silent tears flowed from his tightly closed eyes. He lay there biting his lip and shaking with pain. They were all dressed in varying shades of the same kind of warm spring jacket, long cargo pants and mud-encrusted sneakers.

Brian murmured to the boy on the ground, examining him with reassuring efficiency. "Someone tell me what happened," he said over his shoulder.

"He thought if he stood on the top of the rocks, he could see the whole valley and maybe see if anybody was looking for us," a small boy with longish brown hair piped up.

"I told him not to climb up there," a tall preteen said. She gauged his age about that of the injured boy. His superior attitude reminded her of Brian at that age, but the casual style of his blond hair and height reminded her of her brother, Jim.

"But he did see them, Adam," that same boy with the brown hair said. She judged this one to be around eleven but a little small for his age. "Hey, mister, where's the other guy Dan says he saw?" he added.

Joy tried not to flinch, wishing just once someone would see her feminine side when she wasn't wearing a dress, especially since she didn't wear one often. Then, warming her heart, Brian said in a matter-of-fact tone, "Actually, that was a very tall, very pretty lady, son. And she should be along any moment. Like your friend Dan here, she's hurt."

"Are you here to take us home?" a very small blonde asked.

"That's the plan, son."

Brian was startled when his statement was met by a round of raucous giggles led by a boy with very close cropped hair. Brian looked up at the child who'd asked the question and blinked. *He* was a *she.* And not anywhere near eleven years old. He guessed seven or eight.

Then, for no reason at all, he knew Joy had caught up to him. He felt her presence. He looked over to the way he'd come to see her limping toward the little girl. She placed her hand on the child's shoulder. Even sick and tired, disheveled and dirty, Joy really was a beautiful woman—the very picture of a nordic beauty. Blond, blue-eyed, long-legged. Like that old secular song that had spurred the women's movement said—strong; invincible. She had indomitable spirit that had kept her going when most people would have begged for rest.

But she was so much more. He saw something he thought few people did. Behind the tough exterior, she was kind-hearted and vulnerable and scared to death. He prayed he hadn't had a hand in making her feel that way.

"Suppose we all introduce ourselves," Joy said with a bright smile. "I'm Joy. This is Brian. He's a doctor and I'm a pilot. Is he all right?" she asked him. She'd taken her sunglasses off now that they were in the deep shade and again her concern for the injured boy was reflected in her bluer than blue eyes.

Brian glanced at Dan, then back up at her. "His leg's broken. That's all from what I can see but it's enough." He looked at the other kids and shook his head a little, hoping she got his signal. The break was bad. The other kids, though not presenting symptoms of dehydration thanks to recent weather making water plentiful, were too thin and weak to hike up the mountain. He couldn't imagine they'd had much to eat in the last week and children could lose weight at an alarming rate.

"I think we should get to know each other," Joy said

after a quick nod. "I know you're Adam," she said pointing to the tall blonde. "That's Dan and he got hurt trying to help all of you," she added, acknowledging the boy on the ground whose silent tears had stopped. He stared at Joy with open fascination. Brian couldn't blame him.

Joy kept a bright smile in place when she put her hand on the little girl's shoulder. "And who is this little darling?"

The child with the wispy blond hair and huge brown eyes turned to Joy and looked up. "Oh! You found Bear!" She held up her hands and took the stuffed toy Joy gave her into her thin arms with a fierce hug. "Thank you." She looked around at the boys. "They said the river took her away like it did my daddy. Did you find my daddy, too?"

"Other searchers did and he's doing just fine. As for your bear they were obviously wrong," Joy said, sending them all a censoring look.

Brian stiffened. One of the boys had obviously taken it to be cruel and he was very afraid he might have once done the same thing. It was like having a mirror held up to him that revealed deeds he was now, more than ever, thoroughly ashamed of. He would make amends eventually.

"What's your name, honey?" he asked.

"She's Candy Merrick," the boy with the red hair said. "I'm Chad Fremont and Adam is my big brother."

"I'm Kevin Jaffe," a boy with close cropped brown hair said in a surly tone. Kevin, if Brian didn't miss his guess, was a problem. He figured they'd find out what kind later.

"I'm Mike Cabot. Dan's my brother. I'm sorry I teased you, Candy."

He'd have picked them out as brothers anywhere. They both wore their dark hair long and had the same features. Same stoic forthrightness. Brian put his hand on Dan's shoulder. "Hang tight, Dan. I'll be right back. Try not to move, okay? I'll see if I've got something in my bag for the pain. Have you ever taken a medicine that made you sicker than you were before taking it?" he asked. He was leery about treating a child with pain medication without parental permission, but Dan's leg was definitely broken in two places and it had to be set.

"I don't think I have any allergies. Is that what you needed to know?"

Brian smiled and nodded. Then he stood and propped his hand on his hips as he surveyed the area. There were sleeping bags spread over every available bush drying out in the sunshine. Several backpacks lay in a pile under a tree that shaded a grassy part of the clearing. The rest of the clearing was in the sun and was covered by grass and brush. The stream and banks were littered with storm refuse, giving every indication that it had receded in the past days. It looked like as good a place as any to spend the next few days.

"Now that we all know each other, boys, suppose you get that pad off the top of my pack and help Joy settle down over here by Dan's head. Then I'll have a job for each of you. We're going to camp here for a few days, gain our strength, then see what we can do about getting us all home. How does that sound?"

All the boys nodded but little Candy stepped forward, a pugnacious look on her face. She reminded him so much of Joy at that age. "What about me?" she demanded. "I'm not so little that I can't help. I help all the time when Daddy and Mommy and me go camping."

"Yeah, right. They probably tie you to a tree to keep you from getting lost," Kevin Jaffe sneered.

Joy visibly bristled.

"That'll be enough of that," he said and glared at Kevin, who turned and went with the others. Brian returned his attention to Candy. He didn't know how much help she could be when you measured it against how much danger she could get herself into if they let her out of their sight. Brian glanced at Joy. She merely shrugged but he knew she waited with interest as he debated what to say. Finally he said, "Suppose you collect firewood and bring it over here. You'll be looking for any wood that's lying around dead. But stay within sight of the camp and away from the water. Okay?"

All smiles, Candy skipped off but she stopped and ran back to young Dan. She whispered something in his ear, gave him her bear, then set about her assigned task. Brian grinned, noticing most of what she picked up were twigs. "At least, I'll have plenty of kindling," he muttered.

He heard a chuckle and he looked at Joy. He realized he'd scored a point with her when he saw her bright smile. "You're good with kids," she said. "You made her feel like part of the solution and not a burden."

Brian stared into her pretty face and had to swallow another apology for the damage he was afraid all that childhood teasing had done to her. There was a sadness that lay deep in her soul. He saw it in unguarded moments like this one. She might face each day with confidence and determination but that was in spite of something that burdened her heart. He wished he knew what it was. He wished he knew if he was the cause.

Joy had a stubborn pride that bordered on dangerous, besides that hint of sadness. She still hadn't mentioned her fever and he was nearly sure she wasn't entirely comfortable in the wilderness. There was even a possibility that she'd been willing to face almost certain death to avoid facing that fear in front of him.

He sighed. "It looks as if this crew has been working overtime to make Candy feel like a burden. And some of them have been teasing her unmercifully. My money's on Kevin. I never knew that what seemed like fun for me could hurt you. I said this once before when we were younger, but maybe it needs to be said again. I'm sorry for all the ribbing and practical jokes, Joy. I was a rotten kid."

"Yes, you were." She smiled sadly. "But I usually gave as good as I got, Bri. And I forgave you long ago."

He didn't think she had. Brian also noticed that, as had happened in the past, she hadn't admitted or denied any hurt feelings and added that to his growing list of things he needed to sort out with her. They couldn't go on the way they had been for the past twelve years.

But personal matters between them would have to wait for another time. He had four boys standing around watching them from across the clearing and awaiting instructions. This wasn't the time to debate ancient history and settle up old scores or explore new and troubling insights. That time was quickly approaching, however.

But first he knew he would have to gain her trust.

Chapter Eight

Brian went to where the boys had gathered around his discarded pack and Joy hobbled over to try to keep Dan's mind off the pain. Brian looked back at her, still worried. She sat on the thick black pad and smiled down at Dan. The boy looked up at her as if she were a hero. In many ways, Brian thought she was. He wondered how many men owed their lives to the rescues she'd so boldly executed and how many children owed their lives to her Angel Flights.

He turned away, determined to organize the camp so he could get back to her and make sure she wasn't sicker than he thought. He knelt and looked through his med kit and told the boys, "Check your sleeping bags to see if they're dry. Dan's and Candy's, too. If they are, give them a good shake then zip and roll them. You all know how to do that?"

Chad Fremont nodded and said, "It's the first thing Pastor Harry taught us. We're supposed to do it so nothing crawls in them before we do."

Brian chuckled. "Right. Do you still have the two sleeping bags from your pastor and the boy he jumped in the stream to save?"

"That was Bobby Hood. Dan said we should keep their stuff in case we needed it," his brother Mike said, pride in his tone. "Last night we laid their sleeping bags on the branches of that tree." He pointed to a one-hundred-foot white pine near the steam. "Then we crawled under and stayed dry for almost the whole night." The pine had several low branches that, with the sleeping bags, would have helped form a near perfect roof over their heads.

Ingenious for a kid, Brian thought, but it did mean the bags might not be dry enough for him and Joy to use that night. Luckily, they still had the woolen blankets he'd taken from the plane and the solar blankets from the emergency packs. "It sounds as if Dan is a pretty good leader," Brian told Mike. The boy nodded with enthusiasm. Mike had a substantial case of hero worship for his older brother, much like the one Brian had had for his own brother, Greg.

"Okay then," Brian said, getting back to his instructions. "After you check and handle the bags, I want you to lay out everything you have in your packs so we can take an inventory." He handed them one of the solar blankets. "Use this and go sort the packs out on it, but do it in the sun. If a plane flies overhead, the reflection may signal them. And I mean everything in the packs, kids. Spread it all out so we know what we have. Nothing belongs to any one person except maybe your change of clothes. And if your buddy gets wet and you don't, then you share your clothes, too. We have to pool our resources and pull together as a team."

"Does that include Candy's stupid bear?" Kevin demanded.

Brian glared at the irascible boy. "Actually, Candy already shared her bear with Dan hoping to comfort him. That was very good of her. And, rather than hurt her feelings, Dan took it from her even though I'm sure he didn't need it. She seems to care about that bear a lot. It would be a shame if it got lost again," Brian said pointedly. Kevin looked away guiltily, clearly having gotten the message.

"After that's done," Brian went on, "give Candy help collecting firewood."

"How much should we get?" Chad asked.

"You can't collect too much. Sort it by size and lay it in the sun to dry. We'll be here a while. Make sure you stay in sight of the camp and try to keep an eye on Candy."

Later he'd show them all how to form a human chain in their search for dry wood and other resources. It wouldn't do for anyone to get separated from the group.

"Yeah, we don't want her to get lost again," Kevin said sarcastically and turned away.

Brian let the remark pass. Kevin was a problem he'd need to deal with for more than one reason, but right now it was critical they get organized before night fell.

The boys moved off to handle their chores and Brian returned to Joy and Dan. The next thirty minutes weren't easy and all three of them breathed a sigh of relief once he got Dan's leg set and splinted. The pain medications had begun to dull the boy's agony but he was still lucid enough to clear up a few mysteries. Brian hoped the distraction would help take Dan's mind off the pain, too.

Joy seemed to be on his wavelength because she asked the teen to recount the events that had led them all to where they were presently. Their eyes met and there was another moment of silent communication between Brian and Joy, and he felt his world shift. How could they be so different yet think so much alike? He pondered that while she shifted carefully to recline on her side and propped her head on her bent arm to listen to Dan.

The story that evolved went from good to bad to worse. After a perfect day in the woods, they'd all bedded down in a lean-to. But Candy was a sleepwalker and sometime in the middle of the night she'd wandered away from camp. That had been the pastor's first mistake. He should have set up safeguards against the problem.

Brian began to understand the root of Kevin's antagonism, because when they couldn't find her, the pastor had the kids pack up their meager supplies and took them all off in search of his daughter. As far as Brian was concerned, that was his second strike. He should have gone for help then and there.

It had taken until dark to find her and it had been raining for hours by then. They were all wet and hungry but hiking back out at night would have been too dangerous. They'd taken refuge under the overhang of a cliff but had remained cold and wet all night.

They started their return home the next morning but were blocked because the heavy rains through the night had swollen a creek they'd easily forded the day before.

It was now a swiftly moving torrent. The pastor decided they would stay and camp near the stream that night, but by the next morning the current had only grown swifter and deeper as water flowing down from high country swelled it even more.

That was when the pastor made his third big mistake. Food supplies had already run out. Instead of waiting for the water to recede, Pastor Harry hoped to walk the children out another side of the preserve. But, at that point, he must've been hopelessly turned around. Instead of taking them out, he'd led them deeper into the forest.

When they came to a second swollen stream, they started to follow it since they couldn't safely cross it. Bobby Hood then strayed too close to the crumbling bank. The earth fell away and the stream sucked him in. After a failed rescue attempt with a broken branch, the pastor jumped in to save the boy. The rest of the children tried to follow the stream as he'd told them to, thinking they'd catch up to him.

Unfortunately, the one stream eventually branched into three streams and the next mistake was Dan and Adam's, but it was hardly surprising. They forded the dwindled stream nearest them and followed the swiftest moving one. Dan and Adam thought the pastor and Bobby would have been pulled along that one or they'd be waiting there for them.

The stream had lead them deeper and deeper into the most remote area of the preserve and by then they were so hopelessly turned around that they began wandering in different directions, hoping to come upon signs of civilization.

Brian glanced at Joy when Dan finished his tale. She had pillowed her head on her good arm and had fallen asleep somewhere in the middle of the boy's explanation. Brian didn't have the heart to wake her.

Dan asked how the pastor had been rescued when they were still so lost. Brian explained what they'd learned from Russ Dempsey and speculated that the fordable stream they'd crossed had probably dwindled to its usual flow after it had swept Bobby and the hapless pastor along.

"How long have you been without food?" he asked the kid. Dan's eyes were also growing heavy now, too, but Brian needed a little more information.

"Almost a week," Dan replied on a yawn. "We heard you could eat bugs but we aren't that desperate yet. Then we saw a plane flying low. It sounded kind of weird and then it crashed. But we saw parachutes. We thought maybe it was someone who could help us. Is that why you're here? That was your plane, right?"

Brian glanced again at Joy, a niggling worry haunting him. There was a frown creasing her brow and flags of color on her cheekbones that he thought had more to do with fever than any short exposure to the sunshine. He needed to confront her soon about her condition but it wasn't time for more penicillin. At least now that they'd located the kids, she could rest and heal a little.

"It was Joy's plane," Brian told Dan, pride for her seeping unconsciously into his voice once again. "I was just the passenger with the binoculars looking for you."

Dan shifted uncomfortably. "Adam found the trail up the mountain, but we got tired halfway up. I guess we messed up pretty bad. Everybody felt really sick after that and then when I tried to climb up the rocks my legs just wouldn't hold me anymore."

Brian squeezed Dan's shoulder. "Don't be so hard on yourself. We found your tracks on that deer trail and followed them here. If we hadn't, we would have wasted hours going down the mountain toward where the plane crashed. It looks like we would have come to a cliff and been stuck. We would have needed to backtrack in order to get off the mountain. I can tell you, son, Joy never would have made it.

"Now suppose you try to rest here with her while your friends and I get this camp in order. It'll all work out. We're in the Lord's hands. He's kept everyone relatively safe so far and He made sure we found each other."

Dan closed his eyes and nodded. Brian found his gaze drawn to Joy. He took one last look at her before forcing himself to get to work on the camp.

A cool sensation woke Joy from a sound sleep. She opened her burning eyes to find Brian wiping her face with a cool cloth. Then she looked down at her arm to make sure it wasn't on fire. She knew she should push his hand away—refuse his ministrations but she felt too heavy. Too leaden to move. As if picking up her head would take an act of Congress.

She stared up at Brian, at his solemn expression— one she had to read by a nearby campfire. She knew that look meant something worrisome but she couldn't quite grasp what.

"Welcome back," he said. "You're pretty sick."

"I'm fine," she assured him.

He pursed his lips and shook his head. "No, you aren't. Not at all. Here. I need you to take these," he said holding out a some pills and a squirt bottle. She decided not to argue. Brian was a doctor and a pretty good one from what she'd heard. If he said she was sick, maybe she was.

"What's wrong with me?"

"It looks like a strep infection settled into that wound on your arm."

She frowned. "I thought you gave me penicillin to keep that from happening."

He smiled, his white teeth gleaming in the firelight. "They called it a wonder drug when it was invented but it can only do so much. Your body needed rest and didn't get it. Now it will. You'll be fine."

Her brain felt like mush. Boiled mush. "Earlier did you say we'd need to stay put here for a few days?"

"Don't go feeling guilty. The kids need the rest, too."

"Of course." Her mind cleared just a little. It was dark. She was in a shelter much like the one he'd built last night. "How did I get in here?"

"I built your shelter right behind where you fell asleep so it was easy to drag you inside on the gurney pad."

She supposed she must really be sick if that hadn't awakened her. Joy gathered her strength and pushed herself up onto the elbow and forearm of her good arm. She looked out at the blazing fire. He'd built it against the pile of boulders Dan had fallen from. The stone reflected the heat back toward her shelter and the rock sparkled like a thousand stars in the night sky.

Fear blossomed. That's what was wrong. She was in

the shelter. It was night. That meant she'd have to spend another long miserable night alone with only wood and cloth between her and an alien world. Last night she'd at least been able to see Brian's shelter across the fire. How far away would he be tonight?

"Where are the kids? Did you build them a shelter? Are you sleeping near them?"

"I cobbled together a bigger shelter the way you suggested. It's next to this one. I'll bunk with the boys and Candy till you're up to watching out for her. We'll be a little crowded but it might be an advantage. Dan and Adam have been tying a shoelace around Candy's ankle and one of the other boys' so she can't sleepwalk again and wander away."

She winced remembering that part of Dan's story, though she must have fallen asleep on the tail end of it. She'd heard enough to know Pastor Harry might be a nice man but he shouldn't be let out without a keeper. "Is it necessary to tie the child up? It seems sort of barbaric."

Brian shrugged. "She isn't exactly tied up but that's what I thought." He leaned back on his elbows with his back to the fire and crossed his ankles. "Then as I was getting them bedded down for the night, she insisted. The poor thing looks at that stupid shoelace like a lifeline."

"I suppose to her it is."

Though his posture was entirely casual he seemed... watchful. "I guess so. Think how afraid she must have been when she woke up wandering through the forest, so far from her father and all alone with no idea how she got where she was."

"I can imagine," Joy said and, of course, she could

imagine that very easily. More easily than Brian knew. More than he ever would if she had her way.

"Kids are surprisingly resilient but I still can't believe she isn't a basket case. Anyway, Mike volunteered to be her safety net tonight. He seems very good with her. I already told them we'd be staying here for a few days till we're all feeling a little better."

"I remember. How are they generally?"

"Dan and Adam are exhausted, but that and Dan's fractures aside, they're in a lot better shape than Mike and Candy. Those two show pretty dramatic weight losses considering how loose their clothes fit. Kevin and Chad are somewhere in the middle. One thing is sure, I have to come up with food for all of us."

Talk about mission impossible. Because Brian's face was in shadow she couldn't read his expression to see if that was a worry to him. "It isn't as if you can go to the grocery store, right?"

"It may not be that big a problem. I'll put together a fishing pole or two in the morning."

"Oh. Right. It isn't as if we have guns and I have to worry about you shooting Bambi, right?"

Brian chuckled. "No, in the present circumstances, that's a little beyond me. We also have enough dehydrated meals for all of us for another two days. If I can come up with some protein to add, we can stretch what we have for several more days. And speaking of eating, suppose I put together something for you, right now."

Her heart thundered. They'd be out there for *several* more days? As in more than a couple, more than a few. *Several* could even mean a week, couldn't it? Joy forced her admittedly feeble mind past her own fear to consider what that meant to the kids. They were still so far from home. She'd failed them so miserably. She shook her head. If she missed a few meals, there'd be more for them. "Not hungry," she told him.

"There are a few packets of soup, too. How about that?"

She really couldn't take his kindness right then. "No. Really. I'm not hungry. Not at all."

Brian sat up and stared down at her, his features once again lit by the fire. He wore his examine-the-bug-under-the-microscope expression. Sometimes, she thought, the man saw too much. And that scared her more than all the miles and miles, and lions and bears, between her and home. She looked away, knowing she wasn't strong enough to hide her feelings.

Sighing, he said, "Then I'll leave the water with you. Call if you need help getting up. I'll be awake a while longer."

He backed out of the shelter leaving Joy to face another night staring into the darkness. At first, when she heard a guitar, Joy thought the fever had affected her mind. But then the random cords coalesced into the notes of one of her favorite hymns and then Brian's voice joined the sweet notes. "How our hearts….long for home," he sang, stunning her with the simple beauty of his voice. She'd heard his brother sing the song that was written by a local minister as he led worship at his church. But she'd never guessed that Brian's voice was every bit as wonderful.

With his voice and the notes of the guitar floating on a brisk April breeze, Joy closed her eyes and prayed for their safety and for the night to pass quickly.

* * *

She jolted awake, trembling uncontrollably, her teeth chattering as keen morning light filtered into the shelter. She'd slept soundly but somehow felt worse for the night spent in blessed oblivion. The chilled air seemed to cut through the shelter and sink into her bones.

The cold had contracted her muscles and the shivering involuntarily vibrated her injured shoulder. Joy cried out in shock as a monstrous jolt of pain rocketed through her.

"Your pretty lady is crying, Doctor Brian," Candy called out, as she scampered away from the mouth of the shelter. In seconds Brian darted inside on his hands and knees.

"I wasn't crying," Joy protested, her mind clearing a little. But even to her own ears the objection sounded inaccurate. She might not be crying but taking even a breath without shouting out again was proving difficult. "So c-c-cold," she told him, then gave her teeth free rein to chatter away.

Brian wasted no time piling a sleeping bag and extra blanket on her. He brought her more penicillin and anti-inflammatories and promised she'd feel better soon.

"I'm s-s-sorry to be s-such a b-bother," she chattered.

"You aren't a bother, Joy."

She sighed. "If you s-say s-so."

Brian raked a hand through his hair and didn't say anything for a long moment. When he did, she wished he'd just kept his mouth shut. "I wish I didn't have the idea that you feel guilty for the crash."

Joy chuckled, a mirthless dry sound she'd hardly had the energy for. She couldn't fight his kindness and the truth at the same time. "I was the pilot, Bri," she managed to get out, the warmth of the sleeping bag seeping into her.

"It wasn't your fault."

"The plane and you were my responsibility," she protested. "You're marooned here because of me."

He sighed. "I was afraid of this. That's misplaced guilt. You don't control the weather. Last I heard that's the Lord's department. And remember that if we hadn't been blown off course and then crashed, the kids would still be out here all alone. We both know we're miles from where anyone thought they'd be. And I'm telling you they didn't have too many more days in them.

"Dan worried that he had made a mistake in trying to climb the mountain yesterday because it just about did them all in. I told him that the Lord is in control. He is, Joy. You saw the valley and the cliffs. If we hadn't followed their trail we'd still be up there.

"Remember Psalm 91—'Because he has set his love upon Me, therefore I will deliver him; I will set him on high, because he has known My name. He shall call upon Me, and I will answer him; I will be with him in trouble; I will deliver him and honor him.'

"We're going to be fine. Yes, we're not in the best shape or position right now, but He knows it and He's in control. The kids were praying for rescue. I don't know about you, but I prayed we'd get to the ground safely. We prayed to find them. He'll continue to honor our prayers for our good. He'll protect us."

Joy nodded and closed her eyes. She took comfort from the promises in the psalm, but she also wished Brian would just go away and leave her alone. She swallowed the aching burn of the tears gathering at the back of her throat. Why, just when she'd have told anyone who asked that Brian meant nothing to her, did he have to explode back into her life and do two of the rottenest things he'd ever done to her? Show himself to be such a good and decent man and still be the kind of man she was all wrong for. She could really hate him for both those things.

If only she weren't so close to admitting she still loved him so much it hurt.

Chapter Nine

Brian watched Joy fight tears. It wasn't good to bottle up emotions the way she did. And, now that he'd spent so much time with her, watching her, admiring her courage and heart, he had to believe that he'd been wrong in his assessment of her early yesterday. She hadn't become hardened by her life, she'd just gotten better at hiding her feelings.

Why did she always feel she had to act so tough? Since he was currently acting as her doctor and she'd hidden the deterioration of her condition from him, it seemed a reasonable question to ask. Joy's fever-glazed eyes narrowed and Brian wondered if he'd be sorry he asked.

"I can't believe you asked me that. You, of all people. You're the one person outside my family who I ever opened up to emotionally and you tried to use my feelings against me."

A sick feeling of dread washed over Brian. "Me?" He was to blame? "How did I ever try to use your feelings against you?"

"You tried to make me become someone I wasn't. Someone I didn't want to be. Couldn't be. You knew I loved you. You told me you loved me. Then you told me to change. You told me I had to give up my dream."

"I did not try to make you into someone you weren't," he protested a little hotly. "I wanted to give you a good life. The kind of life my father gave my mother. Maybe even a better one—a better house in a better neighborhood. Certainly a better life than the hard working life your mom had." He threw up his hands. "Shoot me. I'm a rotten person. I wanted to make you happy."

Brian realized she'd stopped shivering when she put her good arm out of the covers and said, "Except that your idea of making me happy would have made me miserable. What about my career? You made me feel as if it wasn't as important as yours and that I'd fail at it. The last thing you said to me after I told you to have a nice life was that you doubted mine would last very long."

He thought back to that day. She'd looked so cool and above the pain he was feeling, that he'd lashed out. Only now did he understand how good she must have already been at hiding her emotions. Only now did he remember his mother telling him Joy showed pain through anger. Had she been hurt all those years and not only angry?

He was about to apologize when she went on, her voice a little raw and the content a little rambling. "And you thought you should get to decide what a good life for me was. I didn't want the life your mother had. I wanted to be me. I wanted you to love me for who I was, not who you thought you could make me into." She squinted at him, trying to keep her eyes open. "And, hey, what was the matter with my mother's life, anyway? She loved my father. She loves us and she loves what she does."

"No, Joy. She doesn't love hairdressing. I heard her more than once sitting in our kitchen complaining about sore feet, aching hands and rude customers to name a few things. She said if your father made more money, she'd quit that salon in a New York minute."

Joy frowned as if trying to process what he'd said, then oddly, she giggled. He didn't think he'd ever heard her giggle. Joy just wasn't a giggler. Then she affected a purposely thick Philadelphia accent. "Do you know what Mrs. Giurastante wanted today? Hair like wire and she wants it fluffy. She wants it fluffy, let her buy a wig. Woman's lucky she doesn't walk out every week looking like she has a steel wool pad on her head."

Brian laughed at her perfect imitation of Anna Lovell. "Then you knew she wasn't happy?"

"She loves her job but no job's perfect. You didn't sound all that happy with being a doctor yesterday. I imagine there are times when your feet hurt after operating all day just like my mom's do. As for the Mrs. Giurastantes of the world, I once had a guy charter my plane who was so rude I invited him off the plane."

"That seems reasonable," he said mildly, trying to look serious while waiting for a punch line. She didn't disappoint.

Again she giggled, making him smile in spite of himself. "We were at ten thousand feet at the time."

"Oh."

"And I love my life. Do sore feet and kids looking at you like the enemy mean you hate yours?"

"No. I wouldn't be anything else," Brian admitted. She'd made her point.

Agitated, Joy kicked away her covers, her fever clearly still raging. Brian was thankful the kids were occupied at the stream fishing so he had the time to take care of her for a while. He reached for the piece of cloth and the water he'd left next to her the night before. After soaking the rag, he swiped it carefully over her cheeks and forehead hoping to cool her down. She closed her eyes and sighed.

"Joy, why didn't you tell me how I'd made you feel?"

Her eyes flew open and she stared at him, confusion wrinkling her brow. "Maybe I should have but why did I need to? Why did I need to defend my plans? Why didn't you believe in me as much as I believed in you?"

He honestly didn't know and that shamed him. He'd failed her so miserably. He wanted her trust—trust in more than his ability to keep her safe on the trail. He'd begun to want her to trust him with her feelings. And he didn't see how she'd ever be able to trust him that way again. Brian realized at that moment how grateful he was for the opportunity to take care of her and he thanked God for it. It seemed he had a lot to make up for.

"I'm sorry sounds pretty lame," Brian told her. "Especially since I keep having to apologize. I know this is late but please believe that I never wanted to hurt you, and that I very much respect you and what you've chosen to do with your life."

She nodded and closed her eyes. "I'm so hot again," she groaned. "And tired."

"I know," he whispered as he continued to bathe her face and neck with the cool water. "The penicillin will kick in soon. Try to rest. That's the best thing for you."

For the next several minutes, Brian watched her as she gradually relaxed and sleep took over her features. Regret and guilt weighed him down. He'd never meant to scar her as he apparently had. He continued to bathe her face for a while then folded the rag and laid it on her forehead. He had to check on the boys and Candy and see if they'd caught any fish for lunch. Breakfast had been the last of the protein bars from the emergency packs. But, as he left, Brian looked back and silently made her a promise. He would never again make the mistake of making Joy think she had to prove herself to him in any way. And somehow he'd make sure she knew it.

The children were all still at the stream where he'd left them attempting to fish with the rods he'd cobbled together out of branches and the plastic string and hooks from the emergency packs. Adam, Mike and Chad were fishing quietly.

As he approached, he realized none of the kids had seen him coming. He was incensed to hear Kevin taunting Candy. "Doctor Brian's going to leave you behind when we go to the plane if you don't start pulling your weight."

"No, he won't," Candy insisted, her face growing red.

"He said we all had to do equal work," Kevin told her, smirking.

"I worked hard." Candy's deep brown eyes glittered. "Harder than you did."

Kevin crossed his arms and looked down her nose at her. "You just collected twigs. We found all the firewood."

"I hate you!" Candy shouted.

Kevin's eyes actually sparkled as if he was proud of himself and that took Brian aback, though he wasn't yet sure why. What he was sure of was that he didn't want to let Kevin's mean-spirited taunts go on any longer. "Actually, Kev," he said before the boy could come up with more ways to mentally torture the seven-year-old, "I couldn't have started the fire without Candy's kindling. Sometimes little things can be very important."

Brian walked to Candy and went down on one knee, putting his hands on her shoulders. He wanted her to feel protected without injuring her pride. She reminded him so much of Joy sometimes. "Candy, will you do me a big favor? Would you go over to the camp and watch out for Joy and Dan for me? If Joy gets cold or starts to sweat a lot, come get me. Or if she wakes up and needs help. Same with Dan. Okay?"

Candy's brown eyes widened. "That'd be like being their nurse!" She nodded vigorously. "I can do that. I can do that real good and be a big help."

"Good girl, you certainly will be a big help. Run along now and I'll see you in a little while," Brian promised and watched her tear across the clearing, then stop short before crawling quietly into the big shelter to check on her first patient.

Without looking at Kevin, Brian casually asked, "Why do you tease Candy?"

"I don't know. It's fun I guess. And nothing's been fun on this trip so far, that's for sure."

"Well, let's sit down and figure it out." He gestured a way upstream to a couple of rocks. "You know it isn't nice," he said as he settled across from Kevin. "Right?"

"It isn't like I'm hitting her," Kevin protested.

"But it isn't as if you're being kind either. I noticed your bracelet. You've all got them. W.W.J.D. What does that mean to you?"

"What Would Jesus Do," Kevin said. "We're supposed to do things like He would. Pastor Harry gave them to us when we started this stupid trip. It's dumb. I can't change water into wine, or feed us all from that lousy fish Adam caught, so how can I do things like He would? He's God and I'm just a kid."

"Well, no. You can't perform miracles but you can still do good things. How do you think Jesus would treat Joy?"

Kevin stared at him, his freckled nose wrinkled in thought. "You mean *Candy.* How would Jesus treat *Candy?* Right? You said Joy."

Brian blinked. Had he really said Joy instead of Candy? Yes, he had. Brian didn't go in for a lot of psychobabble but that felt like a king-sized Freudian slip to him. "Right. I guess I'm worried about Joy's fever," he said, but he had to wonder what else could have made him make such a slip of the tongue. "I've been thinking about her a lot," he added truthfully.

"'Cause she's hurt and sick and your friend?"

It was Brian's turn to only shrug in answer. She was hurt and sick but not his friend anymore. "So, how would Jesus treat Candy?" he asked, making sure to get it right this time.

Watching the way Kevin treated Candy was like having a mirror held up to a period of his life that Brian couldn't brag about. Especially thinking of Joy and how her early life had apparently formed her stoic personality.

And worse, he thought, he was beginning to see something else in the dynamic between the children. Candy was young and female so she was naturally odd man out just as Joy had been in school and the neighborhood and by virtue of being tall, a tomboy and a cop's daughter.

The Cabot and Fremont kids tended to hang together. Among the two sets of siblings, the two older boys were of a like age as were the two younger ones. Dan was back at camp sleeping in the shelter but last night it had been obvious that Kevin had slept where he did, on Brian's far side, because no one had thought to ask him to bed down next to them. Brian had been left out among the neighborhood boys because of his love of books and school and he'd endured a lot of ribbing in a city public school because of his good grades. Like Brian, Kevin must feel left out and pretty bad about himself.

That spark of pride he'd seen in Kevin's eyes when Candy got upset seemed to indicate that making Candy feel badly about herself made Kevin feel better about himself. An uneasy feeling moved through Brian. How had he never seen it before? He'd spent years bolstering his own ego at the expense of Joy's. He'd been right earlier. He *had* been a rotten kid.

Pushing personal thoughts away for later self-examination, Brian eyed Kevin. "You're kind of quiet, Kev. So what do you think?"

Kevin grimaced. "I don't think Jesus would tease her," the boy admitted.

"Why? Besides that it's wrong, I mean."

Kevin shrugged. "I don't know. It's mean maybe?"

"Sure is. Then why do you do it? Because the others don't include you? Does seeing her react to your teasing make you feel better?"

"Maybe. I guess."

"Suppose you try doing something constructive to help you feel good about yourself instead of hurting a little girl. That isn't very manly, is it?" Kevin shrugged again and looked at the ground, clearly ashamed of himself. "Do you want me to talk to the brothers about including you more?"

"No, I'm a real klutz. I'd just get in their way." Slump-shouldered, the boy stood and started to walk away.

"We still need more wood. We'll be here for a few days," Brian suggested.

Kevin nodded. "Yeah. Maybe I'll get more wood. There's still plenty out there."

"Good. Just keep the camp in sight," he reminded the boy as he watched him dig into the task for a few minutes. With Kevin redirected, Brian walked downstream to the fishing trio, who were having only moderate success.

While the boys concentrated on their fishing, Brian turned his thoughts toward the disturbing epiphany he'd just had. He wished he could deny the truth but it was right there staring at him. And what was harder was knowing that he'd had a hand in creating in Joy the need to prove her worth by taking chances with her life. It was a little hard to take on top of learning his teasing of her in their childhood was part of the reason she still went through life hiding behind a facade of false bravado.

He glanced at the camp. "Keep up the good work, kids," he said with a wave and headed back to check on his patients. He'd have laughed aloud if he wasn't afraid to insult his new nurse. Candy had helped Joy move out of the shelter and into the light. She'd settled against one of the boulders that dotted the clearing. He'd created a monster if the way the child was fretting over them was any indication.

"Dan, can I get you more water?" she asked solicitously.

"Doctor Brian," Dan called out when they made eye contact. "Rescue us from Nurse Candy. Please," he all but begged.

Brian chuckled.

Joy looked up from staring into the fire and saw that Brian had returned to camp. He was leaning against the pile of boulders grinning from ear to ear at Dan's comment. She was eternally grateful for the presence of both the children. She couldn't believe she'd told him all the things she'd kept hidden for years. Why couldn't the fever have silenced her tongue instead of loosening it?

"Dan's just being crabby," Joy said and forced herself to laugh. "Nurse Candy has been a great comfort."

"I'm glad to hear it," Brian said. He snatched Candy up and swung her around, then set her down with a laugh. "Will you three be okay here for while? I need to start looking into other sources of protein."

"Isn't the fishing going well?" Joy asked, secretly afraid to ask what he meant by protein. She looked toward the stream. "They certainly seem intent on their efforts over there."

Brian glanced toward the boys. "It's fine for now but I'm afraid to count on fish alone. It could get scarce. I'm not sure they can catch two meals a day for all of us for the three days I think we need to be here. I want to go out into the forest and see what's available. Keep an eye on them, will you? And Kevin. He's collecting wood. I promise I won't be gone past lunch."

Joy saluted Brian smartly and he shot her a pained grin before returning one of his own. She watched him amble off and disappear into the brush. Something about the exchange bothered her but though she felt more clearheaded, what it was eluded her.

Kevin came into the camp then and drew her attention. She noticed him trip as he dropped an armload of wood by the small pile that was already there. He left again and returned quite often with his arms full, but she noticed the boy often tripped over small obstacles he seemed not to notice until it was too late. She invited him over a few times but he was obsessed with pleasing Brian by collecting a mountainous quantity of wood.

Finally, when Joy noticed him straying farther and

farther from camp, she began to get nervous that he'd become lost. She called him over and asked him to keep her company, then sent Candy to ask the fishermen how they were doing catching lunch.

Kevin obediently settled next to her but he fidgeted nervously and pushed his finger against the bridge of his nose. It wasn't the first time she'd noticed the gesture. "Kevin, do you normally wear glasses?" she asked.

With a shrug Kevin pulled a pair of broken glasses from his pocket and gave them to her. The lenses were thick and Joy could see the boy really needed them. And there was no reason he should be without them. There'd been some tape in the emergency pack meant for just this sort of problem. She'd have them fixed up in no time at all.

"Go on over there and get the tape out of the red box in one of the emergency packs. I have just the thing to get these up and running. So what happened?"

Kevin bounded across the clearing, snatched up the red case and brought it back with him. Handing it to her he explained, "Candy stepped on them when she wandered away that first night."

"Oh dear, I guess you have several reasons to be angry with her."

Kevin chewed on his lip, looked up, looked down, fumbled with his fingers and said, "But Doctor Brian says I shouldn't be mean to her."

"I suppose Doctor Brian is right. So are you going to be nice to her?"

He answered with a shrug. "Suppose so."

"Well, I'm very proud of you. And I know Brian

will appreciate all the wood you collected. It'll make his job much easier."

"He's worried about you. 'Cause you're hurt and sick and his friend," Kevin said importantly.

She was Brian's friend? Well, that was news to her. She'd thought what they had going was a wary truce for the purpose of their survival and the children's. While she had to admit being his friend again held a certain appeal, she saw in it a certain amount of danger.

Danger more perilous than anything nature could toss her way. Danger to her heart.

Because she wasn't sure she could let down her guard even that much and not love him again. Because she knew she was all wrong for him. Because he needed a different type of woman—a committee-leading, party-giving, Susy homemaker type—the perfect doctor's wife.

And Joy Anna Lovell couldn't be any of those things and still be who she was. The problem was, she just might be tempted to try.

Chapter Ten

Joy watched Chad and Kevin scamper across the clearing to the stream. Dan was lying on a litter Brian had devised, and Adam supervised today's fishing effort. The sky above was bright as a new dime. Fluffy clouds floated across the not so distant mountaintops and a warm breeze blew the smoke from the fire away from her for a change. All in all, except that the nearest house was nowhere in sight, it wasn't a bad day. She wished this was just a nice picnic she was on.

She'd ventured as far as the glittering stream herself a few times and had even fished this morning. Sleeping in the shelter was easier, proving, she guessed, that the human psyche could get used to anything. And though she had come to appreciate the rugged beauty of the preserve, she still wasn't comfortable being out there.

She glanced toward her and Candy's shelter, where the little girl had fallen asleep, worn out by another day of overenthusiastic nursing. Once again, on this third day since finding the children, Brian had asked Joy to keep the children in sight and had headed across the valley to the mountain. Until that morning they'd been able to catch enough fish to sustain them through each day. The children had grown strong on the protein the fish provided. But the meager number they'd had for breakfast had sent Brian off to implement whatever emergency plan he'd come up with that first day.

With time to do nothing but think and heal these last two days after hiking down the mountain to find the kids, she'd finally realized what had bothered her about Brian's departure that first morning at the camp. It was the way he'd taken such deliberate care to let her know how long he expected to be gone. Had he anticipated her being suspicious that he might try to go to the plane alone? Or had she given her fear away? For which reason had he been trying to reassure her?

Even with time to ponder that disquieting idea and to watch Brian for any sign that he knew the depth of her fear, she had come to no conclusion. The man could hide his thoughts as well as a clam. And she wasn't unaware of the way he watched her. Even at night across the campfire as he sang and played the old beat-up guitar of Pastor Harry's that the children had carried with them on their desperate trek, she felt his eyes on her. It seemed as if he'd no longer use such information against her but she was still leery of giving away too much of herself to him anyway.

Just then the boys waved to someone—she assumed Brian. Aside from a certain lack of elation, she knew it couldn't be anyone else. Pastor Harry had brought along a small cassette player/radio that was now out of juice.

Listening to the news during the few minutes Brian had eked out of it had made it painfully clear that while the eight of them were national news, the rescue parties were searching the wrong areas and moving farther away rather than nearer.

Moments later Joy heard a rustling in the bushes beyond the boulders and campfire. "Brian," she called, "I assume that's you?"

"Be right there," he replied, then came around the tall pile of boulders that stood behind the campfire. Hanging from his hand by their ears were two rabbits. Two very still and limp rabbits.

Joy stared in abject horror. She swallowed with a little difficulty. "Instead of killing Bambi, you killed Thumper?"

Brian looked down at them and winced. "Don't. Okay? I feel bad enough already. The great and happy hunter I'm not. But the kids need nourishing food and it's too early in the year to forage for anything edible. If we're going to start off tomorrow, we all need two more good meals under our belts."

"I know. I know. But can't you try to disguise what they are? You may not get those kids to eat them. Especially Candy."

He looked at the rabbits again and then at her. "It isn't like I have a big stew pot. I can't cut the meat off the bone with nothing to cook it in. I have to do them on a spit and they're going to look like what they are."

She held up her hand. "Hey, I'm just saying...."

He sighed. "I'll do my best. After that we'll all just have to deal," Brian grumbled and stalked off toward the stream and the boys. She watched his slightly slumped shoulders and his almost tentative stride. He certainly didn't look in the least happy to have hunted down those rabbits. She knew the moment the boys knew Brian was there by the way all of them almost came to attention before showing off their catch. Then she knew exactly when they noticed his. From the gestures and their distant chatter, it sounded more as if they were excited than horrified.

So much for their sensibilities. "Boys! Thirty-four or thirteen, they're all the same," she groused.

"Did Doctor Brian really kill Thumper?" a small, horrified voice asked from within the shelter a few minutes later.

Uh-oh. Joy automatically thought of Candy's thin body and the dull look she'd had in her eyes the day she and Brian had happened upon the children. Candy looked so much better but Brian was right. These children, especially Candy, would never make it up the mountain without a few last nourishing meals.

Born of desperation on how to handle the problem of rabbits for dinner, her mind called up a memory. The story about an ex-president and wild hare. She wouldn't lie but she might be able to confuse the subject enough so Candy would find Brian's dinner offering more acceptable.

Joy patted the ground next to her. "Come here, sweetie. I was just teasing Doctor Brian."

"Like Kevin used to tease me?"

Except that I started doing it in self-defense. "Sort of, but in a friendly way," Joy admitted, then changed the subject. "Did you ever hear the story of President

Jimmy Carter and the day he was attacked by a ferocious wild hare while he was on vacation? And was that hare ever vicious! You wouldn't have believed it could happen, what with all the Secret Service protection a president has. But that hare was so determined that he swam out to the president's canoe to get him."

Candy, eyes wide, sucked in a horrified breath. "Did he hurt President Jimmy?"

Injecting just the right tone of shock, Joy said, "The poor man had to beat that hare off with his canoe paddle. And did you know hares just happened to look a whole lot like rabbits?"

"They do? Oh!" She laughed. "Doctor Brian didn't killed Thumper. Thumper is a rabbit."

"Thumper was in the *Bambi* movie, right?" Joy asked, evading the subject.

"Oh, I love Thumper," Candy exclaimed. "But you don't think there are hares out there now that might want to get us, do you?"

"I'm sure we're perfectly safe from the hares."

"Oh, good. I'm going to tell the boys about President Jimmy and the hare and that Doctor Brian didn't kill Thumper. I'll be right back. Don't you go anywhere. You shouldn't walk on your sore leg yet till Doctor Brian says. Okay?"

Joy looked toward the stream and winced. Brian was no longer there. She was at a loss as to how to dissuade Candy from telling her tale and blowing the lid off the rabbit/hare cover story, but then it was too late. Candy was off and running.

Just then Joy heard Brian's chuckle coming from

behind the boulders again. "Now that was treading close to the line between lying and the truth."

"Stop sneaking up on me! You've been doing it for two days."

"I'm not trying to sneak up on you. You just keep sending your mind off to some distant planet or something."

Joy felt her guard go up. *It's you messing with my mind, pal, but you'll never know it. That befuddled I'm not.* "Whatever. And I never once actually lied to Candy. I just redirected her attention with an important historical story."

"Important historical story? Right," he said mocking the very idea. "The famous president and the hare story."

She stuck her nose in the air. "I always thought it was a fact that was rather indicative of the times."

He snorted at that. "Lucky for you, I'd already warned the boys not to identify our dinner to her. I'm sure they'll listen politely and let it ride. Even Kevin. He's really come far."

"Phew. That was close. I was afraid they might set her straight. Yucky as dinner sounds, she needs to eat it."

"Yucky?" Brian grinned. "I can see you never ate my mom's hasenpfeffer."

Joy pursed her lips, annoyed at herself suddenly for not being able to ignore him. He'd developed a tan that made his chocolate eyes look bright somehow and the sun had added more bright highlights to his golden hair. The wind pulled at it now, tousling it and making it glint in the crisp sunlight. Why did he have to be so handsome that he drew her attention whenever he was around?

And why did he have to be so nice? It was so much easier to remember the painful parts of their past when he'd been mean and annoying and to keep her distance. She was emotionally exhausted after the three days of trying to pretend complete disinterest.

"I was spared the hasenpfeffer," she replied, her tone purposely and perfectly sarcastic.

Rather than bristle, Brian just chuckled. "And I always thought you were so adventurous. You don't know what you missed." Brian shook his head and glanced toward the boys. "Kevin's glasses are really holding up well," he said and settled next to her. "I can't get over how you noticed and I completely missed the fact that he couldn't see. I examined him for pity sake."

"It isn't as if you had an eye chart. You were looking at their general health, not the way they see."

"I know but I'm supposed to be a doctor."

She guessed it was more her perception of Kevin's problem instead that bothered him. "The only reason I noticed was that my cousin was forever pushing his glasses up his nose when we were kids. And when he tried to play without them he tripped a lot."

Joy shifted her position, but her discomfort was more about Brian's proximity than the feel of the boulder against her back or any lingering soreness from her injuries. Unless she was walking she had no more pain and even that was now at a manageable stage. "I noticed the unmistakable symptoms is all," she said, forcing her mind to think of things other than a growing attraction to a man who would only bring heartbreak.

Making herself face the truth about the kind of life he wanted, she added, "It looks as if you really got through to Kevin about teasing Candy. This morning after you left he even invited her to fish with him. You'll make a wonderful father one day. When are you going to pick out one of the bevy of beauties you date from the hospital and get serious with her?"

Brian stared at her for long uncomfortable moment. She was sorry she'd said anything so personal. She was just trying to give herself a reality check. After what Kevin reported Brian had said about being her friend, she'd really hoped there was a possibility of building a friendship between them. It appeared she wasn't any better at friendship than she'd been at romance. "I'm sorry. That was out of line," she said.

He blinked as if he'd lost track of the lengthening silence. "No. No, it wasn't. Don't be silly. It's just that I don't have an answer. I'm close to one." He shook his head. "But not yet," he finished cryptically.

That surprised her. Brian always had all the answers.

"How about you?" he asked, his expression searching. "Are you going to spend the rest of your life alone?"

She didn't take as much time as him to answer, but blurted out, "It seems safer. I'm not very good at relationships. Case in point, you and I."

Horrified by what she'd revealed, she watched Brian's eyes narrow, but not in anger—in even deeper thought. He frowned and said, "I don't get it. Since when do you take safety into consideration in anything you do?"

It was anger that made her answer, "Since an engagement ring came with so many strings that I thought I'd strangle on them. Since I found out a heart takes years to mend and not weeks or months like physical injuries. I may be a slow starter, but I learn my lessons quickly."

Hearing his worst fears confirmed in such a bald statement nearly took Brian's breath away. He had no reply except to apologize once again but, before he could, he realized more needed to be said. "I never meant to hurt you, Joy. And I'm really beginning to believe you never meant to hurt me, either. I *did* love you and I think you loved me, too. Neither of us would have stayed so bitter all these years and wary of involvement with other people if we hadn't."

Joy eyed him, almost suspiciously. "Come on, Brian. Aside from the legion of women you've taken out two or three times, I know of three different women who you dated seriously. Your mother expected an engagement any day. Three times. Then it would suddenly be over. It looked like a pattern from where I sat. I felt sorry for them. Each one of them. Because I knew how they felt."

Thinking back on those relationships he now understood the reason they hadn't worked out better. And it was a pretty frightening realization—Joy may have ruined him for any other woman. "They were your polar opposites. Did you know that?" he asked carefully.

She shot him a sardonic, crooked little grin. "It was a little hard to miss. Petite, dark-haired and prissy. Were any of them even over five-foot tall?"

Brian felt himself grow a little warm in spite of a

brisk breeze. "Maybe an inch or two over." He'd been an idiot. No. Scratch that. He'd been a *blind* idiot. "When it turned out you didn't want the things I did, I went looking for your opposite. It seemed like a safer and more intelligent way to approach the problem.

"Maria Baker was a sweet woman. In fact, she was so eager to please that she couldn't make a move unless I told her what to do. Pretty soon her lack of independence started to drive me crazy." Maria hadn't had an independent bone in her body. Check off one of Joy's annoying traits and on to the next. "Then there was Justine Houston."

"The one your mother called Miss High-and-Mighty?"

Brian tilted his head trying to gauge the truth of what she'd said. This was Joy. Of course it was the truth. "Did she? She never let on. But I can't disagree with her. Fashion, home decorating, how to throw the perfect party and what my next career step should be were all she talked about. She was certainly always perfectly dressed and she helped arrange a couple of dinner parties for me. They were a great success and all my colleagues thought she was perfect for me. It was a while before I wised up. But I didn't care where hemlines were or if blue was the decorating color of the year. I mean, did I know French country decor from early American, or more important, did I care? As for my career, I just want to save lives. Young lives in immediate jeopardy. In short, she bored me to tears and started really aggravating me in the way she pushed me to get involved in hospital politics." So scratch the consummate doctor's wife he'd wanted, but that Joy never would be.

Joy raised an eyebrow and confirmed his worst fear. "None of that is anything the rest of us didn't see coming. And everyone who cared about you breathed a sigh of relief when you broke it off." Which meant everyone had known what an idiot he'd been that time. "But whatever happened to Rebecca Southern? I've known her for years from her work in the ER. She's so sweet."

"Becca wanted all the things I did. But I realized that while she wanted the same life I did, I was only a means to an end for her. And frankly that's all she was for me. In the end, I decided I should at least love my wife and that she should at least love me. Becca and I weren't in love. We were in like."

What hadn't worked was that none of them were Joy even though they'd each partially fit his image of the right doctor's wife. He was tempted to just blurt out— she wasn't you. He restrained himself. It was too late for thoughts like that.

"Without love, marriage would be a recipe for disaster," Joy said. Her expression filled with something he couldn't name. He hoped it wasn't pity.

"Exactly," he said quietly. "Marriage and love have to go hand in hand. You and I had love, but different goals. Maybe our youth and inexperience were the problem. We loved each other so much that we never talked about important stuff like the future and our specific plans and needs. We each assumed we knew. And it didn't help that I was so dead set on what I thought was the good life—the life I wanted—that I couldn't see another way to live."

Joy stared at him for long moment. "Are you saying you don't want the house in the suburbs, the wife who lives for her kids and to support your career?"

He turned toward her and looked into her lovely face. "I don't know. I wish I had an answer," he whispered, drawn to her in a way he'd never felt with another woman. And so he made his biggest mistake since agreeing to sub for Zack Stevens on the Angel Flight. He leaned forward, tipped her chin up and kissed her.

And she kissed him back.

If his brain had made a bad decision, his body made the next. He pulled her closer and deepened the kiss. In the next split second, Brian retreated like a scalded cat. He was not going there. Not with Joy. He'd let those feelings rule his head once before and had barely escaped with his heart still beating. He turned away, raked a hand through his hair and averted his eyes. He didn't want to see what he felt reflected in her sapphire eyes or he might make a second mistake and it might just destroy both of them.

He stood and started away. "I'd better get the fish cleaned and cooked. It's well past noon." Something compelled him to stop—to turn back. "Like I said, I'm always apologizing. I'm sorry. That was completely out of line." He dared to focus on her face then. On the look in her eyes. If the eyes were truly the windows of the soul, Joy's were no less tortured than his. What was he doing to both of them?

Chapter Eleven

Brian stared down at the fish he'd just cleaned. He winced and stilled his hands. Mutilated was more like it. No one would mistake him for a surgeon at that moment. He'd attacked the poor dead thing as if it were the author of all his confusion. The fish, however, was blameless. Brian wasn't.

He should never have kissed her.

What on earth was the matter with him? He'd had his life completely planned since he was fifteen. And he'd hit every mark. National merit scholar in high school. Valedictorian of his college class. Top one percent of his medical school. An internship and residency at a top Philadelphia hospital. Even the endorsement of *Philadelphia Magazine* for the past two years as the area's top pediatric trauma surgeon.

The only part of his plans to ever derail had been in his personal life. He was supposed to have been married by now to a sophisticated woman who was nonetheless a lot like his nurturing mother and maybe even have had a couple of children. Yet that had never materialized. From where he stood at this moment, his feelings for Joy were the cause. He was very much afraid that the insight he'd had back at the camp was all too true.

Joy really had ruined him for anyone else.

She was everything he admired. Intelligent, brave, independent and tenacious. And none of the things his mother had been—meek, gentle and compliant. She was also a few things a mother just couldn't be. Headstrong, reckless and prone to tempting death on a regular basis.

He'd been terrified for her more times in the past twelve years than he could count. It wasn't that he didn't admire her for the people she'd rescued, the homes she'd helped save or the environmental disasters she'd helped avert. Even if she were interested in having children, he didn't want his children's mother losing her life and leaving them orphaned. He didn't want that heartbreak for himself, either.

The trouble was, he'd only just realized that if Joy did die in one of her daredevil escapades, he'd be no less devastated for their lack of a current relationship. He may as well just admit it to himself. He loved her—had probably never stopped loving her.

In the last three days they had talked about a lot of issues, and their opinions on everything from world affairs to movie trends to the kind of food they liked were practically identical. Sharing little chores and big decisions on the welfare of these children, whose lives had suddenly been placed in their care had lightened a burden that could have been overwhelming. He'd also come to see how very lonely his life had become.

So now what, Lord? Why did You put us here together? Am I here to reconcile with her or get her out of my system? If it's that, I can tell You one thing. It isn't working. I know this wasn't an accident. You must have a plan. You always have a plan. So how about letting this thickheaded guy in on what it is?

"Brian," Joy said from behind him. "Dan was fooling with the radio. There was enough juice left in it to get a weather forecast. A Noreaster is headed this way. They're warning of flash floods. It looks like really heavy rain by tonight. What do we do?"

He turned and stared at her. She stood framed by the blue sky, the clear sparkling stream and the misty mountain at the end of the wide valley. Her spiky blond hair fluttered in the breeze. Her eyes matched the sky behind her and shimmered more brilliantly than the glistening stream. And his heart just about seized in his chest.

How can I love her so much, Lord, and not be able to find a way to have a future with her? Now his heart pounded. *Is that my answer? Find a way? You want me to look for a loophole in my life plan? It* is *mine after all.*

If the sun could have brightened, it did. Was this why he was there? Brian almost felt dizzy.

It isn't supposed to be my plan is it, Lord? It's supposed to be Yours.

Had he learned nothing from his brother Greg's foray into police work after their brother's death of a drug overdose? As an undercover narcotics officer, his big-hearted brother had descended into the depths of despair, nearly losing his way before he'd finally realized that in trying to avenge Tommy's death, he'd ignored God's call to the ministry.

Had Brian also ignored a plan God had for him? And if Joy was a part of that plan, how much would he have to alter what he'd thought he wanted? He shouldn't take the time now to think about all this, but it was an insight to seriously consider. Something he was probably supposed to consider. He blinked.

"Bri, did you hear me?" Joy demanded. "What do we do? Even with those stupid disposable ponchos from the emergency kits, the kids'll get wet, and how will we cook if we can't light a fire?"

He tried but he couldn't get his mind off the possibilities his discovery opened up. After the crash he'd begun to want Joy's trust because he knew it was safer. Then he'd wanted her friendship because he was sick of the arguments and animosity. Now he might want more, but maybe friendship was the place they should have started years ago and maybe it was where they could start now.

Looking back he could see that love between them had appeared in full bloom, but it had not been cultivated on a strong foundation. So for right now her friendship and trust would be a good place to start. More might or might not follow, but it was a journey long overdue. "Will you trust me?" he asked.

When she looked at him as if he'd lost his mind, Brian almost shouted for joy—no pun intended. Then she added, "You've done a great job getting us this far and taking care of us all. What's not to trust?"

He almost sighed. Not what he'd meant but better than a sharp stick in the eye. Maybe personal trust would follow. Like the trek up the mountain, he and Joy had a personal journey to make. He had no idea what trail either would eventually follow or if they'd end up together when the real world intruded, but at least it was a beginning.

Joy wondered what was going on in Brian's head. She'd dreaded even seeing him after that astonishing kiss. But then Dan had flipped on the radio wondering if it would work since they'd let the batteries rest to recoup some of their power. The forecaster's voice warning of a Noreaster had floated across the camp like an ill wind. The children's faces had frozen in varying expressions of trepidation.

And so, for their sake, she'd forced herself to seek out Brian. She'd gained courage from her own need to get to the plane so she could get away from him. It was what she wanted, she told herself, ignoring the pain the thought caused her.

That was how it had to be.

Since finding the boys and Candy, they had traded stories, the occasional joke or memory of their childhoods around the camp fire at night and during the long afternoons. They were the products of the same neighborhood and both Christians so they often agreed on moral and lifestyle issues. But she also knew he still believed, as he had years ago, that women should not mix marriage and a career. And it was that fundamental difference that made them all wrong for each other.

She wanted a husband and children but the man

would need to be someone who could support her love of flying and her vision for Agape Air. Joy had no intention of ever endangering the lives of her unborn children by flying into dangerous situations. She might even give up rescue work once there were children depending on her. But she also saw no reason to give up being a pilot altogether or to give up running the company she'd helped her uncle build.

When she'd joined Agape, Uncle George had owned four small cargo planes and had employed two other pilots. Since she'd taken over as CEO, she'd helped build it into a thriving company with a fleet of commuter and cargo planes powered by both prop and jet power plants. They now employed nearly two dozen people and were responsible for the travel needs of quite a few local corporations.

It didn't seem to Joy that the Lord would've granted such favor to Agape Air in the years since she took over the everyday operations if he didn't intend her to continue as its head.

It was for that reason she had to assume she and Brian were only meant to nod politely when forced into each other's company. That kiss had shown her that even a friendship between them wouldn't work because all of their lives, every time they got too close, one or both of them walked away wounded.

She didn't know about Brian, but she knew saying goodbye and going back to her life was going to be tremendously painful this time, too. More so now. And she was sick of being hurt by him. She was sick of hurting him, too.

If only he hadn't kissed her. If only she hadn't kissed him back. The kiss had thrown her so far off balance that she hadn't thought about her answer to his question about trust. She'd answered without thinking, and only after assuring him that she trusted him had she suddenly been positive he'd meant something completely unrelated to wilderness survival. She was afraid to imagine what and so she relegated it, and the kiss, to the back burner of her mind and forced herself to listen to his plans for the trip to the plane.

"We'll cook up all the fish and the rabbits and start off as soon as possible. I don't want to be down here if that stream starts rising. There's a lot of recent damage to the grass through this whole area that tells me all this was under water this time last week and those were just freak thunderstorms. We'll camp at dark. Hopefully we'll get to the crash site and have a camp set up before the rain hits. It's the best we can do. I'll finish cleaning these. Suppose you help the kids stow what you can in their backpacks. Try to divide it all according to their weight. I'll carry what you don't think they should." She nodded and went to turn away. "And, Joy," he said evenly, "don't even think of putting a pack together for yourself. You'll have enough with just your injuries as a handicap without a pack hanging on that shoulder."

"But won't you and Adam have to carry Dan, too?"

He nodded. "I still don't want him trying to use cobbled-together crutches. It's bad enough you have to."

"I'm fine," she automatically said. He had enough to worry about with Dan and the other children.

He winced, then smiled sort of sadly. "No, you aren't. You're just better than you were and I appreciate your not wanting me to worry, but I will anyway. Adam and I will be fine so don't you worry about us. He and I have talked it over."

Uncomfortable with his apt reading of her, Joy retreated to the camp without another word and got the kids working. Two hours later they left the valley behind, Brian and Adam in the lead, with Dan on the litter. Yesterday, after having Joy point out the area where she thought the plane had gone down, Brian had scouted ahead and marked the beginnings of the easiest trail upward he'd been able to find.

They traversed the valley and Joy's stomach knotted as it hadn't in days when they approached the dark forbidding tree line. The canopy had thickened in the days since the crash and it seemed to swallow up all the sparkling sunshine of the valley. It looked like another world and only prayer gave her the courage to step into the shadow of the tall, tall trees.

The trail, another deer track, rose steadily and, though clear of the tangled undergrowth that bordered the path, it was not easy going with her injuries. Joy was exhausted by the time they'd gone a mile onto the mountain. And they had at least three thousand vertical feet and many, many miles of trail to cover. This was their only hope for a quick rescue though, so Joy trudged on, praying for strength with every step. The strength to go on. The strength to say goodbye to Brian when they reached their goal. The strength to survive the inevitable loneliness.

Soon the sky beyond the vivid green canopy darkened and turned the color of lead. Five hours after
they'd set out, the rain started. It was way ahead of the
estimate. They became aware of it as a noise high up in
the trees—a gentle and quiet rustling accompanied by
the tangy scent of spring rain. The aroma engulfed them
just before the moisture reached the ground.

Joy and Brian quickly helped everyone into the
flimsy emergency ponchos and tossed two of the solar
blankets over Dan, hoping to keep him and the litter dry.
But the ponchos tore easily on the prickly underbrush
at the sides of the trail so they were all soon uncomfortably damp. They trudged ever upward, through the
steady, wearing rain. It chilled to the bone. The temperature fell, too, and though the rain had begun slowly, it
increased in volume and was soon much heavier.

Then the trail turned slippery under foot. The hard
packed ground beneath a heavy layer of loam turned to
mud. The top layer often broke loose and slid from under their feet, pitching them to the ground. The loam,
while cushioning their falls, had a thick musty odor of
decaying plant material and was anything but pleasant.

Brian looked back at a moment when both Joy and
Candy went down. He traded places with Chad and
Kevin at the front of the litter and hiked back down the
trail to scoop Candy up into his arms. His affection for
the little girl was plain. He asked if Joy thought she
could make it. She didn't at that moment, but she got
to her feet and forced herself to grin and nod. She made
a production of wiping her filthy hands on her sodden
slacks and declining any assistance. She didn't want

him helping her—touching her. After that kiss—that haunting kiss—it would be too much.

Knowing Brian was watching her closely, Joy tried not to let on that she was near the end of her endurance. Her hand was blistered, her underarm was raw and her crutch tip kept sinking into the ground, jolting her. It threw her off balance and slowed her progress markedly. She'd fallen quite a bit behind when Brian stopped and turned to check on her. He called to Mike, who had been chattering to Dan to keep his mind off the pain the jolting trip caused in his leg. Mike returned down the trail as Brian set Candy down and took her hand, helping the little girl keep up with the litter.

"I'm fine," Joy called to Brian and waved him on. But he started back down the trail to get her.

"Come on, honey, I can see you aren't okay," he said reasonably and blocked the trail with his body. She tried to go around him but he reached out to still her, his hands spanning her waist. "You need help."

He held on and she could feel him willing her to look into his eyes. She looked up and had to blink back tears. He cared. He really did. And that made the whole situation so much worse. She didn't blame him anymore. He couldn't help what he needed from a woman anymore than she could help not being able to be what he needed. They were who they were. And what they were.

Wrong for each other.

Chapter Twelve

Brian knew the second Joy realized how he'd come to feel about her, and not because her defiant expression changed. It didn't. Her eyes lit with fire, she said, "Don't, Brian. It's no good and you know it."

"I don't know what I know—except that I need you to start trusting me again. Just try. And let me help you. I can't stand seeing you struggling and in pain."

"No."

"Why not? I'm not going to make fun of you for needing help. I can't go back and change what a rotten kid I was. That's in the past. I can only promise not to do it again. Please. Let me help you."

She bit her lip and nodded. So without another word, he took the crutch and slid to her side to brace her hip against his, taking the weight off her knee and ankle. Then after circling her waist with his arm, she nodded and he started them moving forward. The boys and Candy were a good way ahead, having continued trudging on without them.

Their little troop made slow but steady progress. And the rain just kept on coming down. The trail soon looked more like a murky stream and the footing got even worse. Candy quickly tired again so Brian hoisted her onto his other hip and carried her, too. His arms felt as if they were breaking by the time an early dusk fell thanks to the heavy storm clouds that hung somewhere overhead above the treetops. And if he felt that bad, he didn't want to think how the others felt, Joy at his side or the boys carrying Dan.

At last they broke through the trees into a meadow that was bordered on two sides by forested land. Ahead, directly across the meadow, rose a foreboding, almost perpendicular wall of rock. To the right the land seemed to fall away. It was as if they'd arrived on a terrace in the sky.

A terrace Brian was very afraid went nowhere.

He'd thought this would be the level where they'd find the plane. They'd been headed for a hole in the canopy like this one, but mountain trails were deceptive and could wind you around a mountain as easily as take you straight upward.

Brian let go of Joy and handed her the crutch, trying to hide his worry as best he could. "Wait here," he said putting Candy on the ground next to Joy. "I'll be right back."

He jogged across the meadow, his feet splashing in puddles created by the day's torrential downpour, the pack on his back chafing his shoulders. As he drew closer to the end of the meadow, he slowed his pace and his heart sank. The land didn't just fall away gently. It fell off abruptly into a cliff as steep as the one that boarded the meadow. Brian looked over the edge. Though he couldn't see anything because a thick, gray fog floated just below his feet, he knew it was a long way down.

The din of the heavy rainfall rose up in a nearly deafening echo from the deep crevasse before him. He backed away. Shaken. Dispirited. Unless the deer track continued somewhere through the forest off to the left of where he'd left Joy and the kids, he'd brought them all this way for nothing.

Had there been another way to the area where Joy had seen the plane going down? A way not accessible from where they were now?

With a heavy heart, Brian turned back the way he'd come, but his gaze fell on the towering cliff that rose above him. And then, as if it had been carved just for them, he saw a dark blotch in the cliff wall hiding behind a web of vines. Drawn to it, he hoped and prayed it was a cave. A sanctuary for the night.

He had to pull down the network of vines that guarded the five-foot-high entrance. Though the tendrils holding them to the rock gave way easily enough, the effort still pulled open the new skin growing over the blisters he'd gotten climbing the tree to rescue Joy days ago.

Once the entrance was clear, Brian carelessly wiped his hand on his wet slacks, leaving a trail of blood. He wondered absently what his colleagues would think of his triage technique if they could see him now. With a careless chuckle Brian unhooked the flashlight from his pack, anxious to explore his find. He had to duck, hunching his shoulders as he moved forward at the mouth of the cave. After about six feet, the five-foot-high entrance opened up into a wide, deep cavern with about a twenty-to-thirty-foot ceiling. The deafening roar of the storm suddenly faded. Inside the haven, the raging storm felt like a distant memory.

Brian flicked his flashlight into every corner of the large room, relieved to find it was uninhabited by any winged or four-footed creatures. Although, someone had camped in there at one time leaving the remains of an old campfire and some leftover wood stacked against one of the walls. Which was fortunate since any wood they might have found that day would never burn. He took a deep experimental breath and found the air relatively fresh thanks to a slight draft that flowed through the cave. That meant a fire wouldn't smoke up the cavern.

His next breath was a relieved sigh. The cave would be a sanctuary from the storm and it was certainly a gift from God. "Thank you, Lord, for delivering us," he said, dropping his pack.

As quickly as possible, Brian started a fire to light the way through the entrance tunnel and into the cavern. The kids and Joy couldn't get much wetter, after all, but the cave could warm up while he went to get them.

Minutes later Brian hurried back out into the storm to shepherd Joy and the kids to the welcome safety and comfort of the cave. The rain was so heavy when he emerged that at first he couldn't see them across the meadow. The wind had picked up and temperature was dropping rapidly, too. The rain felt like icy needles striking his face as he sprinted toward where he'd left them. Heart pounding, Brian dashed across the field only spotting them when he was yards away.

"There's…a cave," he called breathlessly, motioning them forward. He reached them and, after taking Adam's pack, pointed the boys in the right direction, though he could no longer see their promised sanctuary through the downpour and swirling fog.

He'd just about reached Joy when lightning split the leaden sky, spearing toward the ground just beyond where the meadow abruptly fell off the end of the terrace. The ground shook as the bolt struck the bedrock of the cliff below the meadow. Its accompanying thunder rolled toward them with a deafening roar. Candy squealed in fear and ran toward him, practically leaping into his arms.

Brian cradled her head against his shoulder and smiled sadly at Joy as he stepped to her side. He wasn't taking no for answer. She was dead on her feet and the sodden earth of the meadow would never support her crutch tip. She needed him.

"Where did you go?" she wanted to know, thankfully not arguing the point, but falling into their earlier rhythm next to him. "It looked like the rain had swallowed you up. You just disappeared halfway across the meadow."

She sounded worried and it made him grin in spite of his exhaustion and discomfort. "I found a cave. I built a fire and we can warm up, dry off. In a few minutes we'll all be high and dry and comfortable."

"Aren't there bears in caves?" she asked, missing a beat in her steady if uneven gate.

"And bats," Candy added, helpfully.

"Bats?" Joy's head snapped to stare up at him, rain lashing her face. She had to squint because of the heavy downpour but he could still read fear in her narrowed eyes.

"Don't worry. We aren't dispossessing any furry creatures from their home. I didn't see evidence of any wildlife at all. We won't be the first people to camp there, though. Someone else was through here and even left firewood. They seem to have stayed there without incident. The wood they left should see us through the night. No animal would likely come near with the smell of a fire. I promise, ladies."

It wasn't until they reached the mouth of the cave that Brian suspected how very afraid Joy was. She stopped dead in her tracks. He put Candy down and the child ran toward the campfire. "Take the ponchos off before you go near the fire," he shouted, then turned to Joy.

"It's okay. I checked it out. It'll be fine."

He'd felt her stiffen and her spine went rigid. "Of course it will." She put her crutch under her arm and started forward alone.

Brian felt such despair at that moment that he was tempted to give up trying to find out whether the Lord had sent them there to find each other or get over each other. But as he'd come to believe, if all this was part of the Lord's plan, he had to find the answers he was supposed to or risk misery for the rest of his life.

Using Dan's litter as a screen, Brian set up a private

place for every one to take turns changing into the clothes they'd washed and dried while in the valley. Luckily Harry Merrick had packed not only an extra pair of jeans and a shirt, but a pair of sweats to sleep in according to the boys. He gave the sweats to Joy and changed into the other clothes the pastor had worn that first day.

With everyone warm and dry, they ate the already cooked fish they'd brought along and then settled in for the night. Brian took out the pastor's guitar and played a few praise tunes he'd taught the kids. The hymns always seemed to settle them down at night, and one by one, exhausted from the difficult day, their sweet voices faded as they each relaxed into sleep.

He'd surreptitiously watched Joy since they'd arrived at the cave. While she did sing along, she'd hardly moved a muscle from the moment she'd settled on a sleeping bag next to the campfire. Now, he realized that waves of tension rolled off her. He walked over, crossed his ankles and sank down next to the fire, facing her.

"Want to talk about it?" he asked.

She looked up from the fire. "Talk about what?" she almost snapped.

He shrugged. "Whatever you want. How about that I missed you all these years?"

"Run out of puppies to kick?" she asked sardonically.

Please, Lord, give me the words You want me to say. "Okay," he said reasonably. "Maybe I deserved that. Let's talk about it. You've told me I'm forgiven but it keeps coming up. The sad part is that I never knew why I teased you. Until you were fourteen I didn't even know the things I'd said hurt you. My mother pointed it out and, after sulking because she'd ruined my fun, I realized she might be right, so I quit doing it."

"I'd always wondered why the insults stopped."

"I really hadn't realized it did more than make you mad. The odd thing is that until I saw the way Kevin treated Candy and the look in his eyes when she reacted, I never even knew why I'd done it all those years. Now I'm feeling ashamed all over again."

"It was a long time ago," she said, staring at the fire, then she angled her head to look at him. "But just out of curiosity, why did you?"

Brian reached over and set another log on the fire. "I fed my ego by making you feel less than you were."

Now she stared openly, her disbelief plain to see even in the low light of the cave. "You? Brian, you've been brilliant your entire life. How could you need help with your ego? Especially from me. I was at best a B student."

He winced but was determined to come clean. "My brilliance as you call it, set me apart. And it wasn't that I felt inferior to you. No, I was a lot more cowardly than that. I was older so I felt superior already. You were an easy mark. It was simple to get a rise out of you. An easy victory, you see. You'd get upset and confirm my vast superiority."

Joy frowned and stared into the flames. "Bri? Why bring this up now? I thought we'd forgiven each other a long time ago for all those stupid battles."

"I know you said you had, but then we broke up and I think all the anger came back."

She stared at him for a long moment then sighed. "Thus the kick-the-puppy statement a little bit ago. Okay. You're sorry. I'm sorry. That's the end of it."

He took her hand and ran his thumb over the back. "I hope so because I really have missed being your friend. But I've hated being your enemy even more. And since realizing how much all those years probably formed who you are, and how much my lack of confidence in your abilities hurt you, I've been thinking that all the wild, daredevil chances you've taken might have been your way of proving yourself. If anything happens to you because of me, I don't know what I'll do."

Joy could feel her heart stutter. She couldn't do it. She couldn't be his friend. Not with love for him just about choking her in an effort to reveal itself. But how could she say no and not give her feelings away? His touch was just too much on top of his honesty.

"I told you before I don't have a death wish," she said flippantly, taking her hand back. "And I don't take as many chances as you think I do. I'm a good pilot and I know my limitations. But if it'll make you feel better, we'll be friends so you'll know I'm not taking chances." She'd just avoid him the way she'd done for most of the last twelve years. It was something she'd grown quite adept at.

"Then how about you start trusting me," he said, pinning her with a shrewd look. "Tell me what's wrong. What's been wrong since before we bailed out? Why did I practically have to shove you into this cave?"

So he did know! She shrugged sheepishly. They hadn't even gotten off the mountain before he'd seen the truth. He wouldn't have belittled her for her fear, but she had kept it from him and only now did she realized she'd done it to use as a buffer.

But this cave, with its dark walls and dank smells, must have dissolved all her stubborn intentions. This was just too much. She felt as if the walls were creeping ever closer out of the darkness just beyond the circle of light cast by the campfire. "I'm afraid," she said, her shaking voice betraying the depth of her terror.

"Joy, its perfectly safe. This cavern has probably been here since Noah was sitting at his drawing board."

She clenched her hands together and shook her head almost violently. "Don't you see. I don't *do* this. I fly *over* this. I rescue people *from* this. I drop smoke jumpers *into* this and fire retardant *on* this. I don't sleep in it! Not in shelters or in caves. And I sure don't get licked by baby bears or eat cute little bunnies for dinner." Her voice broke and she swallowed hard. "I just want to go home!"

Brian nodded and scooted closer, then squeezed her good shoulder, clearly trying to comfort her. "I thought so. I'm sorry you didn't feel you could trust me enough to confide in me because of the way I treated you when we were kids. I'm sorry you didn't think you could count on my friendship."

As always, Brian's kindness made her throat ache and her eyes burn. This was getting dangerous. "We haven't been friends for a long time."

He pursed his lips and nodded. Then he made it even more dangerous. "I still want to be your friend, Joy, but I think I want a lot more, too."

She shook her head again. "I can't be what you need. I don't see how, Brian."

He sighed. "I'm not sure I do, either. But I don't think we ever forgot each other. I don't think the anger would still have been between us when we started this trip if we had. And I also think the Lord had a message for us in all this. I think it's why we're here."

She tried to glare at him but couldn't muster any anger. Not when he sounded so convinced that the Lord had been working in their lives. But she wasn't entirely convinced, either. Did he really believe what he'd said? If so, he'd certainly changed his mind from the other day. "I thought you said we were here to rescue the kids. That we were thrown off course because we were meant to find them."

"They could just as easily have been somewhere else if that was His only purpose. You could have insisted we go to Piseco to pick up a trained spotter. Go back further. Zack Stevens could have been the flight physician. Kip Webster could have stayed healthy one more day and been the Angel Flight pilot. I think the Lord is talking to us. I know He's been talking to me.

"Why I teased you isn't the only thing I've learned about myself these last days. We talked about why I didn't marry Becca or Justine or Maria. I gave you a list of reasons why those relationships didn't work out. Each one of them had qualities that are important to me. Yet those qualities drove me nuts in Justine and Maria and I couldn't even force myself to love Becca, who was perfect for me on paper. The truth is, Joy, those relationships didn't work out because they weren't *you*—no matter how perfectly they were suited to be a doctor's wife."

"Please don't do this," she begged, her voice shaking with the strain. "I can't be what you want, Bri. Don't you—" She looked into his eyes then, and stopped. She knew what was coming but she couldn't bring herself to stop him from saying it. In some masochistic corner of her heart, she wanted to hear it once more.

Just one more time.

"Maybe I just want you to be *you*. Maybe that's enough. I don't think I ever stopped loving you, Joy."

She looked at him, longing all but choking her. The firelight flickered over his chiseled features. She forced herself to be strong. "No. I wouldn't be enough and you know it. We'd be fine together for a while, then you'd be sorry. You'd feel cheated and you'd resent the things I couldn't give you. Please don't do this. I can't go there again. I can't hope and have it fall apart again." Exhaustion and sadness weighted on her heart like lead.

Just then Candy sat up screaming that a bear had come into the cave. Brian rushed across the cave to scoop her into his arms and assured her she'd just had a bad dream. Watching him, Joy's heart broke that he wouldn't be the father of her children. She held out her arms for him to settle the whimpering child in her lap when he returned.

"We need to get some sleep," she said, exhausted but still fearful. Fearful of more than the cave, now. Fearful that if they didn't get home soon he'd try to wear her down. Fearful that she'd weaken. Fearful of the heartbreak that was sure to follow.

Brian dropped his pack next to her, tossed a sleeping bag open on the ground and sat down on it. Then after leaning back against the pack, he gestured to her and hauled Candy into his lap. He looped an arm around Joy's shoulder and urged her closer, then tucked her head under his chin. "Sleep," he ordered. "I'll keep watch. I won't let anything crawl on you." He grinned sadly. "Or eat either one of my girls."

"I can't be your girl, Brian, and you need sleep, too."

He laid his index fingers on her lips. "Sh-sh. I was an intern. Lots of practice being awake nights. I'm good at it. Got an A in Sleep Deprivation 101." He sighed. "Just go to sleep, honey. There'll be plenty of time to talk tomorrow."

Joy closed her eyes, praying they'd all get home safely—she and Brian with a minimum of heartache.

And that was imperative if she was going to survive with even a portion of her heart intact, because with every minute she spent with him, Joy became more and more brokenhearted that she was so wrong for him. It seemed a cruel reality that they couldn't find a way to be together. Because, if in twelve years her feelings hadn't died, she had no hope they ever would.

Chapter Thirteen

Brian held Joy in his arms for hours with Candy sandwiched between them. He spent the time tossing logs on the fire with his free hand. And thinking. He fantasized about how it would be if Candy were their child and this were just a normal family vacation. It was ironic that he'd had a dream about a family vacation at the start of the trip before ever meeting the child.

He'd discounted it then because he and Joy had still been at loggerheads, and he'd already learned of Joy's dislike of camping—especially as a vacation. Now he knew why she'd felt that way and was glad for the trust she'd placed in him. Then the feeling faded. He might know her much better now but he still didn't think there'd be any family vacations with her, camping or otherwise. She might have finally told him about her fears but there wasn't much of a chance of them ever being a family.

Because she was afraid of trying to, or even hoping they could, work things out. The truth of how badly he'd hurt her all those years ago had finally penetrated his thick skull. Joy, who seemed so fearless most of the time, was terrified of him and what another rejection from him could do to her. And he couldn't even reassure her.

Because he wasn't sure they had a chance, either.

Restless and needing more firewood, Brian eased first Joy then Candy onto the sleeping bags and covered them with a blanket. After adding enough wood to keep the fire going for an hour or two, he took the sleeping bag Candy had been using and the extra blanket and moved into the mouth of the cave. He looked out into the black night. It matched his mood to a T. The rain continued to fall in sheets, blown by fierce winds. The Lord had indeed been good to have kept them safe from the storm. But he felt battered just the same.

He loved her.

But do we try to mesh our lives when we want such different things from life?

Still, he had time to earn her trust and show her that he didn't want to hurt her. That he just wanted to explore their feelings. Seek to find a way for them to be together.

It wasn't as if rescue was imminent, he told himself. They still had to find the plane which—now that they'd somehow wound up on a terrace to nowhere, he realized—might be like trying to find a needle in a haystack.

Brian sighed and rolled on his side. It was probably hours till dawn so he might as well try to sleep. He still had time.

* * *

A blinding shaft of sunlight drilling through his eyelids woke Brian. But the sound of torrential rains still echoed into the cave entrance. It took a minute to get his synapses working. Before he could even move, though, he heard Adam snicker. Brian tossed the blanket off and sat up. He noticed the sleeping bag under him and grinned up at the kid. "You think this is funny?"

"You have to admit Candy goes with the Cinderella theme a whole lot better than you do."

Brian pretended insult. "I'll have you know I wear cartoon-character ties and scrubs all the time. Relaxes the little ones when I go to examine them."

Adam theatrically melted onto on the cartoon-themed sleeping bag and fell into Brian. "I'm relaxed all right," the pre-teen said and laughed. Then he glanced toward the meadow. "So what's up with this? Where's all the noise coming from? It's not raining anymore."

Brian clapped him on the back. "Let's go find out. Just let me go toss some logs on the fire before we go exploring."

"Done. Chad's awake, too. Can he come?"

Brian nodded. "Sure. Grab your brother and I'll meet you both outside."

He stepped down into the beautiful morning still feeling a little disoriented even after viewing what all the noise was about. The sun was so bright he had to shade his eyes. The air was so clear it was as if the rain had scrubbed it clean. The scent of pine and an elusive aroma he couldn't nail down floated in the air. Someone could make a fortune if they could bottle it. He filled his lungs with it again and closed his eyes, silently reciting the prayer he had since that first day after the crash. *Thank You for this day, Lord. See us through it safely.*

"We're all set," young Chad called as they tumbled out of the mouth of the cave entrance. "So what's that noise?"

Brian grinned and stepped aside, gesturing toward the cliff at his back and the spectacular waterfall.

"Wow!" Chad shouted.

"Like, double wow!" the elder Fremont boy breathed reverently.

"I think if we walk to the edge of the meadow we'll see something just as incredible. From what I could tell in the fog, I think this is a horseshoe-shaped canyon. We're on one leg, the falls are on the opposite one. I'm not sure what's below but we're definitely still on the eastern side of the mountain."

"You can tell that because the sun came right into the cave, right?" Adam asked.

"Exactly," Brian said. "Now don't walk too close to the edge," he added and started walking toward the beautiful sight. Even Joy had to appreciate this kind of show. The two boys followed close on his heels toward the spectacular waterfall that cascaded over a tall cliff across the deep horseshoe canyon. Yesterday it had all been so veiled in fog that he couldn't see the falls at the other side or, spreading out far below far to the right, the flooded valley floor.

"Wow!" Chad exclaimed again.

"I'll say," his brother agreed. "It's a good thing we started out when we did."

Brian sent a quick prayer of thanks winging upward for those few moments when that radio had worked, warning them of the impending weather, and added one more for guidance today. Chad went down on his knees then and crept closer to the edge.

"Watch that, son! With all this rain, the edge could be unstable and crumble the way that stream bank did to your friend Bobby."

"Hey, is that the plane we're looking for?" Chad called out and pointed over the edge at the cliff wall on the arch of the horseshoe.

Brian dropped to his knees and stretched out flat so he could safely look over the edge. And stared in horror. An image of Joy, limp and still and wedged in the cockpit of the little powder blue and white plane, flashed across his mind. He put his head down on his arm and closed his eyes, banishing the thought. She hadn't tried to land it. She'd bailed out with him. Joy was sleeping in the cave—safe and out of danger.

He looked back at the wreckage. The front two-thirds of Joy's Cessna was perched precariously on a wide ledge. The left wing had broken off and lay along the cliff over the fuselage. The tail section, wings and cloud logo scratched and bent, had become hung up farther down the craggy cliff on some trees that protruded from the rock. The waterfall thundered down the vertical cliff wall adjacent to where the plane had drilled into it.

Adam had joined him and all three of them observed the twisted wreckage in silence.

"You and Miss Joy were in that?" Adam asked, his voice full of fear.

"We sure were. Lightning went right on through the nose. She lost her electronics but kept the plane in the air until the engine lost its oil pressure. For a while after that, too. Long enough for us to bail out."

"It's pretty wrecked," Chad said in a voice a bit higher than usual and of course a little louder because of the roar of the waterfall.

"It is that," he said and let out a breath he'd forgotten he was holding. Brian felt sweat bead on his forehead. And she'd wanted to try to land somewhere. He shook his head banishing the horrifying vision once again.

"What'cha lookin' at?" Candy chirped loudly from a position a bit higher off the ground near Brian's knees.

Brian's blood went cold and he jumped a foot. Without a thought he rolled to his back, grabbed her and pulled her onto his chest. She giggled, clearly not understanding the danger at all. "Oh, did you ever scare me," Brian told her. He sat up with her and put her in the grass. "Crawl away from the cliff. It's very dangerous here for you. In fact, let's all get back from the edge. Is Joy still asleep?" he wanted to know as soon as he got to his feet.

Candy's arms were anchored to her hips by her bunched fists. "Everybody else is sleeping. I got bored."

Nothing new there. Candy got bored every two minutes it seemed. "Listen, guys, take Candy back and wake Joy. Send her out here to me. Okay?" He needed to tell her about the plane, but more pressing was his need to see her. He just needed a few minutes to get hold of his feelings first.

The boys ran, swinging Candy by her arms between them. Happy just because it wasn't raining and they'd had yet another adventure. Kids. They were so resilient it never ceased to amaze him, even though he saw it every day.

Every day. He did see it every day, but like a lot of things he had and didn't have in his life, he'd begun to take it for granted. Like the smile of a healing girl. Like thank-you pictures drawn by a grateful boy.

Like loneliness.

He sighed. One foot in front of the other. Just get through the day. How long had he been doing that? No wonder getting marooned here with Joy hadn't seemed all that bad until yesterday's trek up the mountain. He wondered what he'd have done if Chad had not found the plane. Would he have waited a day—or two—before "noticing" it. If it weren't for the people back in civilization who were worried about all of them, Brian knew he'd have been tempted.

And all for just a little more time with Joy.

But there were worried parents and other relatives and the plane was down there. And now he had to figure out a way to get to it. And disappointed though he was with the timing, he was grateful the Lord had sent them the message via the radio that they should move from their camp in the valley.

Brian wandered closer to the edge and glanced due east at the valley beyond the lower elevation's tree canopy. He didn't imagine the water in the valley was particularly deep, but moving water didn't need to be deep to be dangerous.

The upper cliff their cave had been carved from was part of the same formation that formed the deep, horseshoe-shaped, east-facing canyon. The waterfall flowed off the upper elevation that lay directly across the canyon from the meadow. It roared downward and into a deep pool, if the darkness of the water below was any indication. Though lower elevation trees hid a stream from view, Brian imagined the falls and pool eventually flowed into the stream they'd camped near.

He followed along the top of the lower cliff onto a crescent-shaped spit of land about twelve feet deep at its apex, but barely three feet deep at its beginning. It curved above the lower part of the canyon where the plane had come to rest. He scraped away a covering of pine needles and found the ground was hard-packed and more like granite dust than dirt. The needles had come from two pines that had rooted in the cliff face. They were the same kind as the ones holding the tail section suspended above the pool—the tail section where Joy had said the transponder could be found.

He heard her call his name from the meadow. "I'm here," he called back. "Wait there." He hastened around the narrow corner to her side. She stared at him, looking wary. Worried. And he knew it had nothing to do with the plane and everything to do with their conversation by the fire the night before.

There's still time. Still hope. When we get home, we'll work it out, he told himself.

"Did the kids tell you?" he asked, needing to break the silence before it became strained.

She blinked and looked away. "That you'd found the plane? Yeah." She looked out over the cannon. "This is the big gap I saw in the trees but I didn't see the cliffs from that vantage point." She turned and looked back at the meadow and groaned.

"Looks different from down here, I imagine," he said, turning to look at the sunlit meadow behind them.

"Don't you see? I could have landed in the meadow if I'd still been behind the controls."

The image from earlier of her in that twisted hulk of metal and broken glass exploded in his brain. "Don't, okay?" he snapped. "What is, *is*. No second-guessing God's mercy." Hand on her shoulder, Brian urged her to turn and walk toward the edge of the cliff. He didn't need to touch her but couldn't seem to help himself. He needed that physical connection to reassure himself that she was really there. Safe. Alive.

More confident of the ground's stability after examining its foundation from the other wall, Brian pointed down and to his left toward the arch of the horseshoe. "I think you're going to have to walk me through getting the transponder up and running."

Joy, of course, couldn't kneel with her knee so banged up. And since walking to the edge on unsteady limbs would have been dangerous, she tossed the crutch to the ground and sat down, albeit awkwardly. Then she rolled to her stomach and scooted to the edge. After peering over it, studying the wreckage for a long moment, she cleared her throat. "It must have come in point-blank at the cliff. That's why the nose is caved in so far and why the windshield is gone. The momentum would have pivoted it to the side that way. The wing would have sheared off and folded back as it slapped sideways into the wall. I'm guessing the stress just snapped the tail off and then it slid down to lodge in those trees." She shook her head and looked like she was honestly tempted to cry. "At least you were insured, baby."

"Joy?" Brian said to call her back as she continued to stare at the wreckage.

"I was thinking," she said, her voice still far away, "did you ever notice how the stuff people leave on their plates goes from being food to garbage in the split second they put down their forks? The plane went from being an asset to trash just as fast."

He cupped his hand on the back of her head. "I'm sorry. I know you hated to lose it but it wasn't worth your life. Nothing is."

"Except getting those kids home."

Brian didn't know what to say so he opted for being practical. "The transponder—"

It was her turn to point, but as she moved to look up at him he had to move his hand. Trying not to feel bereft he looked away from her beautiful face toward the tail section.

"See the stress fracture on the left horizontal stabilizer?" she asked.

"Say what?"

"The stabilizers," she said evenly, "are the horizontal little wings on the tail."

"Okay. That's some more plane jargon to file away." He took a closer look now and saw the crack. The whole assembly was really just barely hanging there. And who knew how long it would stay there without help. "Okay. So first I'll secure it. I'll throw a rope around the…uh…" He made his hand go up and down. "Vertical…um…"

Joy looked sideways at him and grinned. "The vertical stabilizer."

Brian raised an eyebrow and grinned back, holding her gaze. "Well, that follows, at least."

She sobered. "You can't fix the transponder, Bri."

"No!" He wasn't going to let her talk him into anything that included her climbing down there.

Annoyed, Joy turned her head and glanced down into the pool, then shot Brian an impatient look. Hadn't she made it plain all along? This part was her job. She looked back to the plane, a plan formulating. "I can't get down there alone, and climbing down to the tail section would be almost impossible, but if you could lower me, we could do it."

She saw Brian clench his jaw. "What was it you said when you wanted me to bail out without you?" he demanded. "Oh, yes, I remember. 'There is no we in this.' Same here. You aren't in any shape to rappel down a cliff or to scrabble all around in a precariously balanced hunk of torn-up metal that's just barely clinging to the side of a mountain."

Joy rolled to her back and pillowed her head on her good arm. She sighed. Maybe they really were slated to argue into eternity. "And how many transponders have you fixed?"

"None. How many cliffs have you rappelled down?"

"None. How many transponders have you even seen?" she countered with lightning speed. "I'm not excluding your help. We need to do this together."

Brian groaned. "I'm not talking you out of this, am I?" He stared down at her, his dark eyes weary and grave. He was on one knee, his arm propping up the weight of his shoulders. And she knew there was a lot of weight on those shoulders right then. Like her, he was used to having lives depend on his capabilities but not, she thought, seven lives at a time. Sometimes she forgot how hard he'd had to work these last days because he'd made it look effortless. She looked down at his hand that was hanging loosely from the arm leaning on his knee. He'd torn open the blisters again. His beautiful, capable hands were a disaster.

Determined to do her part, Joy looked back up at his face and tried not to see the man she loved, but the man who would eventually have to turn away from her. It didn't work. She couldn't turn off her feelings, so she opted to hide them and do what she had for the last twelve years. It was a lesson she learned from Brian's mother. "Put one foot in front of the other, trust in the Lord and get on with life," Mrs. Peterson had told Joy's mother when asked how she'd gotten through her son's tragic death.

"Did you really think you could talk me out of doing what I have to do?" she asked rhetorically. "You should know me better than that at least. My knee's getting much better. I can bend it now and it almost takes my weight. And my shoulder is a lot less stiff."

"What about your ankle?" he demanded.

"Not as good," she answered truthfully, but quickly extinguished the brightness in his eyes at her admission. "But then you're going to be taking some of my weight off it with the rope. We can do this, Bri. But only if we do it together."

Joy rolled back to her stomach and looked down at the plane again. If only life were as easy as climbing down a cliff and fixing a broken piece of electronics. If only they could go through life the same way.

Together.

Chapter Fourteen

Joy watched for a while as Brian readied the ropes. It was the final step before she hooked up to the complicated apparatus he'd devised to get her down the cliff. Even though Brian was the one who knew how to rappel, and even though she was the one handicapped by injuries, her worry was for him. She had a terrible feeling of impending doom. It made no sense. No sense at all.

She looked out at the crisp, cerulean sky. *Watch out for us, Lord. I think with Your help I'll be able to bear losing him to his regular life, but I have to know he's still out there alive.*

It should be fine, she knew. He'd explained how he would lower her using one of the nylon ropes and rings he'd harvested from one of the parachute harnesses as a crude intimation of a pulley system. Then he'd follow her and secure the tail section.

It sounded, if not easy, then at least not impossible. She smiled, her vision of the Swiss Family's visit to the

Adirondacks was now complete. Brian's "Don't leave anything behind" credo for the preservation of the land had come in handy once again.

He'd stationed the children to watch from the cliff edge at the end of the meadow. Having been a terribly curious child herself, Joy worried about trying to keep them at a distance and Brian agreed. He thought it would be safer to position them to watch rather than risk them trying to approach the cliff later if curiosity got the better of them. It was interesting how often they agreed out there in the middle of nowhere, when the only thing that mattered was survival, especially when the welfare of the children was concerned.

"Ready?" he asked, drawing her back from her thoughts. He took her hands and checked the cloth-wrapping he'd done on her palms and his. She smiled when he looked into her face, remembering how she'd teased him that he was a bit late taping his own. He grinned back clearly remembering, too.

His gaze still locked with hers, he asked, "You're sure you can't talk me through it?"

She looked away and over the edge, wishing she could. Even with Brian's help it was going to be painful, but together there was a better chance of success. She looked back and shook her head.

"You aren't just doing this so I won't think—"

She stopped his words with her fingertips on his lips then gripped his forearm. "I'm scared to death for both of us. Okay? But since I don't know why the transponder isn't sending, I don't see how I could talk you through it. There's no other way."

He pursed his lips and nodded. "Okay then. Here's how we're going to start out." Making a last-minute check, he yanked hard on the line he'd secured to the pine trees that grew from the upper cliff. It was either a lucky break or Divine Providence that the trees had sprung up in a direct line from where the plane had come to rest. She turned toward the high cliff above them and looked up at the trees. Both she and Brian were more comfortable with the idea that the trees were a sign of a heavenly blessing on their foray into mountain climbing.

Brian backed them toward the edge. "I'm going to take you over the edge. I just don't think you can handle going over the edge with that ankle."

There was no way she'd tell him how true that was. She'd been limping around without the crutch for all of ten minutes and her ankle was pretty unhappy.

"Your line will hang slack at first," he explained in a measured tone, "then it'll go taut. After that I'm going to leave you hanging there and go back up over the edge to lower you until you're at the plane." He wrapped his left arm around her from behind. "Got it?"

"Got it," she assured him, trying to ignore his nearness and concentrate on the task at hand. So she continued reciting her part of the plan to focus her mind where it needed to be. "If the plane isn't as far away from the cliff wall as it looks, you'll lower me inside the cockpit through the broken windshield."

"At which point you'll have to be extra careful of broken glass," he reminded her.

She nodded. "If there is room next to the fuselage,

though, you'll lower me right to the ledge aft of the plane. However I get inside, I'll grab the tool kit and get out either on my own steam or you help me back out. Then I wait while you lash the tail section to the trees to stabilize it.

"When you've done that, you'll lower me from your position at the tail section and I'll swing over to it. Once I'm there, I'll slide down inside the tail and do my thing with the transponder."

Brian's arm tightened around her waist. He'd run his line over his shoulder, across his body and under his thigh. He'd be climbing back up without any help but his own strength. "Okay, get ready. Remember, take your weight on your left foot and only balance with your right. Here we go," he said, then he pushed backward and sprang out and over the cliff edge.

The rope slipped between them with an audible zip as they dropped. It was dizzying. Thrilling. Scary as anything she'd ever done except sleep in shelters and caves. Joy grinned. This was nothin' at all after that!

Her line went taut as he'd said it would and the cliff came rushing toward them. But Brian stopped them from crashing into it with his feet as a gust of wind brought with it a cool spray off the falls. "All right. Get ready. I'm going back up," Brian told her as he let go of her and swung off to her side. Then he reached up and pulled himself upward, disappearing over the edge moments later.

Joy was on her own, staring at the cliff. "You know this is kind of cool," she shouted up to him.

"That's my Joyful," he called back with a chuckle in

his voice. "Always the daredevil. Okay. Here we go. Let me know as soon as you can if there's enough space between the cliff and the body of the plane."

Her rope zipped over the edge and she floated downward. Joy looked down as another gust of wind misted her skin with spray from the falls. She shivered and waited anxiously for the moment when she'd have to commit to going in the cargo door entry or have him pull her back up so she could swing over and be lowered into the cockpit. Soon she was behind what was left of the fuselage of the plane, about eight feet off the ground.

"I think I can fit through there. Going in the cargo doorway is going to be a cakewalk," she shouted to him. "Lower away."

"Be careful, Joy," he called to her. "Remember to keep your face to the wall and your rope free of the wreckage as you sidestep. And remember to stick close to the left inside the plane. You don't want to throw the balance off and go over the side with it."

"Not in my plan for the day, pal," she yelled back and looked up as Brian dropped over the side and slid downward toward her.

She looked away, anxious to get this over with. It was the tire from the splintered landing gear that had kept the plane from hugging the wall, she saw now as she moved under the severed wing. Making sure her line didn't get hung up on anything, Joy sidestepped until she reached the open cargo door.

Aft of the doorway, the plane was gone and the underbelly cargo section was crushed nearly flat. The destruction almost took her breath away. She gritted her teeth and stepped inside, experiencing a moment of complete and total unreality. Joy looked through the gaping hole that used to be the rest of the plane just in time to see Brian drop past that level down to where the tail section had landed below the ledge. Wires hung and wavered in the breeze. They looked like the tentacles of a wounded beast seeking redress for its injuries.

Joy lectured herself to stop being fanciful. The Cessna was only a piece of machinery. But it didn't work. Instead, a strange unnameable feeling settled on her. They'd left Agape Field and were supposed to be gone from home for hours, not days. Brian was supposed to have spent half the flight monitoring a patient and the return trip was to be relaxing. She'd seen that day as routine, though it hadn't been in her original plans—a quick and dirty flight and a late dinner at her mom's. Nothing to it.

Except that so much had gone wrong. Sometimes she felt the way Brian did—as if all of this was supposed to happen. She shook her head to clear her mind. She had work to do. It was time to go home and get back to real life.

She grimaced and stepped carefully toward the cockpit. And her foot skidded, sending a painful jolt up her bad leg. She looked down at an Air and Flight magazine she'd been reading as she'd waited in Ogdensburg for Brian to return from the hospital. She picked it up and stuffed it in the partially open backpack she wore. At least she'd have something to read while they waited for rescue and it wouldn't be blowing around to catch her unaware again.

Her heart in her mouth, Joy started forward again and sidled carefully up the center aisle. The tools she needed were stowed in a pouch behind the copilot's seat. She hadn't told Brian they were on the right side of the plane, though. She knew if she had, he'd have insisted on doing this part himself. But she couldn't let him. If the plane tipped and went over the cliff before the transponder was up and sending, the children would need him, not her, in this vast wilderness.

It wasn't that she was being a hero. She'd thought this out. So when the plane rocked upward as the wind rushed up the cliff side and caught the wing, Joy bent over and plucked the case out of the pocket. Then she stood straight and waited for everything to settle down.

"You okay in there?" she heard Brian shout.

When the rocking stopped, she tucked the case into the backpack and turned. "Fine," she yelled, but just then another gust rocked the crippled bird. The floor rose up and slammed into her foot. Pain shot through her ankle and knee. She yelped.

"You *sure* you're okay?" Brian called out again.

"Fine and dandy," she shouted but it sounded strained to even her. Hopefully the roar of the waterfall had muffled her distress. Another rock of the fuselage and she was ready to get out of Dodge.

Brian finished lashing the vertical stabilizer to the trees with the tied-together parachute line he'd salvaged. He gave it a tug, satisfied that everything seemed to be holding, then he climbed out from under it to ascend the cliff. Luckily, this section of the cliff wasn't as vertical as the part above the ledge where the plane rested. Just as he'd climbed back up to the top of the tail section, Joy called that she was in place and ready to be lowered from above.

She grinned as if she were having the time of her life. "You're amazing," he told her when they were right next to each other.

Joy didn't even seem to hear him. She just stared into the tail. Wires and insulation hung from the torn skin and pieces of the stuff took wing every time the wind blew. She giggled, startling him.

"What?" he asked, hungry to understand how her mind worked.

She blinked and seemed to notice that he was next to her. "I was just thinking that I broke your wilderness credo big time. Before I ever set foot in the preserve, I'd already left a major mark on the landscape. This is littering on a grand scale."

Brian let out a crack of laughter. "Are you ready?"

She nodded and turned to let him pull her tool kit out of the backpack as they'd planned. He smacked it against her upturned palm and she tucked it in the waistband of her khakis before stretching out flat on the floor of the tail section that had broken off and slid further down the incline, catching on some trees.

"I'm all set," she said as he untied her rope from the branch he'd tied it to. "Be right back up," Joy promised with a grin, as he let out the rope so she could slide inside the tail.

Brian crawled over. If the tail broke free he wanted to be close at hand to help her anyway he could. Shielding his eyes from the sun, he peered inside to watch her.

Joy had given the impression that she was having fun. He wasn't sure if it was bravado or bravery, but he watched tensely as she picked her way past all sort of debris.

"Can you see it?" he called to her.

"No. The gurney ripped free. I need to move it off the hatch."

"Push it up here to me. I can hold it out of the way."

"No need, I've got it," she told him as she shoved the gurney to the side and rolled over. Then, flipping open a hatch, she reached in with both hands and started fiddling with a bright orange box.

"It definitely wasn't sending. I think the lightning shorted something." She got her tools out and went to work on first one thing, then another, and another. Then she looked up and gave him a thumbs-up sign, smiling brightly. "We're in business," she said.

Joy put her tools in the backpack and shouldered it. He could see the strain on her face as she crawled up to him. He hated this! He'd known this part would hurt her.

"Brace yourself here," he told her when she reached him and he helped her negotiate the jagged edge of the tail. "I'll climb up now and pull you up as you climb."

She nodded and he left her there. That she didn't argue with him was a testament to how difficult the ascent out of the tail section had been for her. He made the climb easily enough. Then Joy fell right in with his rhythm, moving upward on each pull he made with the makeshift pulley system he'd jury-rigged. It was as if they instinctively were a perfect team.

It wasn't long but felt like hours until he was able to

pull her up to join him on the ledge. Brian's arms, so overworked yesterday, were already screaming from the climbing and pulling her up the fifty feet from the tail to the ledge. "Let's rest here a few minutes," he suggested, all but breathless and beginning to doubt that he'd be able to make the climb to the top at all. He wiped the sweat off his forehead with his sleeve. He couldn't keep his hands from shaking.

"Suppose we pull up a hunk of ledge and take a load off our feet—or more specifically that ankle."

She nodded and sat, still a bit awkwardly with her ankle and knee so sore. "So," she said a little breathlessly herself, "that wasn't so bad." But she grinned, telling him she knew just how much the ascent had taken out of him already.

"What was wrong with the transponder?"

"In layman's terms, the automatic relay didn't trip."

He snickered and dropped his head onto the rock wall at his back. "Could you go a bit more layman than that?"

"It didn't turn on. Probably the lightning fried a relay somewhere."

He frowned gravely. "Oh. That would be a big problem." He looked up the cliff and chuckled. "Look." There were six heads peering over the cliff edge at them, all of the kids on their bellies in the grass. "Wave and look invincible so they don't worry."

"Is that how you do it? Pretend? Is all this Swiss Family Robinson stuff just smoke and mirrors? You just pretend to know how to survive out here?"

He frowned, but smiled with his eyes. "Hmm. I was thinking more Gilligan goes to the Adirondacks. Maybe

MacGyver crash-lands. Guess I blew my secret. Good thing help's on the way." He looked at her then, worried about his strength and the climb ahead. "It is on the way. Right?"

"Oh, undoubtedly." She laughed. "And aren't they going to be surprised when they find all of us together?"

Maybe still sitting on this ledge, Brian thought as he looked again at the sheer cliff above his head. "From the news reports we heard before the radio quit on us they'll be surprised all right. Have you thought much about our families?"

Joy winced. "I've tried not to. Mom went through so much losing Dad the way she did. She must be worried sick. Your dad and mom already lost a child and they almost lost Greg twice. This is probably even worse on them."

He agreed, especially considering his dad's weak heart. "They must all be so worried. And can you imagine the guilt Harry Merrick must be suffering, having lost not just his kid but the other five, too."

She wiped her hands on her thighs. "Oh, I want a bath."

Brian pointed to the waterfall. "Well, there's a shower over there. I promise not to look."

She wacked him on the shoulder and the kids up on the cliff egged her on even though they couldn't hear the conversation.

He cupped his hands around his mouth and called up to them. "Thanks a lot, you guys. Now that they're finally coming for us, you turn on me. I guess you don't need me anymore."

There was much giggling up on the top of the cliff

and assurances of complete and total loyalty. "Are you guys coming up soon?" Dan called down to them. "Candy's bored." And they all cracked up again.

She shook her head. "Such a difference from the kids we found," Joy said.

Brian put his arm around her shoulder and stared at her. If the kids weren't watching he'd never have been able to keep from kissing her again. She was so beautiful, even with mussed hair, a smear of dirt on her face and windburned cheeks. She was such a puzzle to him. He wished he understood her. "You've been great with them, you know," he told her, still feeling the lack of that kiss. "You're really wasted as a pilot when you could be such a great mother."

He didn't know what he'd said at first, but her eyes flared in anger and she pushed away from his embrace. "You really are a chauvinist, do you know that? Can you imagine how you'd feel if I said to you, 'You'd be such a great father. Too bad you wasted your time becoming a surgeon.' That's the difference between you and me. I don't think I can only be one or the other. And here's something to think about while you sit here alone. Where in the Bible did it ever say women can't work outside the home?"

She got to her feet and walked along the ledge toward the plane, which continued to rock every time the wind rushed up the cliff walls.

"Joy! Wait! Come on. We need to talk about this."

She looked back, her eyes hot in her fury. "No, we don't, Brian. We have absolutely nothing to talk about. Nothing at all. I don't think we ever did."

He got to his feet now, too, and shouted after her. "You shouldn't go near the plane the way the wind's kicking up. It was bad enough when it was necessary."

"Maybe it's necessary now just so I can get away from you."

What if she got hurt because he'd stuck his foot in his mouth…again! "Look, I'm sorry. That was out of line. It was a compliment. It just didn't come out the way I meant it."

"There's nothing else you could have meant. And why I still care about your opinion, I can't imagine. You're obviously still living in the dark ages."

He held his hand out to her. He didn't want to follow her and push her closer toward the plane than she was already. She was a good ten or twelve feet away from him—almost to the plane already. "Just please come back," he called as she turned away again.

Slow motion.

He'd always heard that during sudden life-changing events, time slowed to a crawl for those involved. And it seemed he'd heard right. Brian watched in horror as the ledge between him and Joy fell away. The rock just sheered off from about four feet above where she had stood only seconds before.

Joy backed up, her mouth forming a silent scream. Brian felt the end of her line run through his fingers and realized that if the ledge went and he didn't have a good hold on it, she'd fall. She was staring up at the line and he understood her distress as she realized he'd dropped it. He leaned toward the dangling rope.

Brian heard a noise and started to look back over his

shoulder, and sucked in a startled breath as the earth moved under his feet. Then a crushing weight enveloped him and a heavy blackness welled up from somewhere below. The air left his lungs with a sickening force. Surrendering to the blackness felt better than continuing to battle the force crushing out his very existence.

Chapter Fifteen

Joy heard herself scream Brian's name and at the same time it echoed from the children up on the cliff. Brian had looked utterly shocked when the rock from above him sheered off and came down on him. And only as it was happening had she understood that he had been reaching for her lost lifeline. If he'd seen the danger he was in, he'd had no time to react, because he'd been thinking of her.

She grabbed the bright yellow nylon rope when it completed another arc back toward her. She looked up at the second rope. Brian's line was tangled in the pile of rock covering him and several feet of the ledge between them had sheered off. There was also every chance the part of the ledge where Brian lay buried could go at any moment, especially considering the added weight of all that rock.

The kids up on the cliff called down demanding to know what they could do to help. Joy didn't see what they could do. *She* didn't know how to help. Her mind had gone blank of anything but the racing thoughts of complete and utter panic. "Give me a minute to think," she shouted back.

"Give me a minute to pray," she sobbed quietly. She did and the clamor of panicked thoughts faded away. She found she could focus. Then she just acted.

Joy swung out over the precipice knowing seconds counted as she grabbed for Brian's rope while holding hers taut and bracing her feet on the wall above the rubble. Then, carefully, she pushed away from the wall and landed on the ledge. The ledge held.

Hardly noticing her bad knee screaming in pain, Joy knelt and called Brian's name. His legs didn't move and he was buried under the rubble from his chest to his head. She tied both his line and hers to his belt in case the ledge let go. If it did, her weight would pull him upward, hopefully sending him to the top of the cliff where the children could pull him to safety. She refused to think of where that would leave her.

Then, rock by rock, she uncovered him, tossing the refuse of the collapse over the edge into the pool below, rolling the pieces too heavy to lift over the edge. She kept calling Brian's name and ordering him to live—to not even think of dying no matter how much he hurt.

Brian never moved, but when she put her hand on his chest she could tell he was breathing, though shallowly. She sobbed in relief then uncovered the arm and hand he'd had stretched out to grab her lifeline. The arm and wrist looked badly broken, bent at an unnatural angle.

Joy kept digging.

When she'd tossed all the rock over the edge, freeing him and hopefully taking the strain off the ledge, she prepared to deal with his arm. Joy had every faith that the transponder would draw the rescuers, but Brian's arm had to be stabilized before they could transport him. She remembered the Air and Flight magazine she'd picked up in the plane and pulled her backpack off to get at it. Then she unwound the long length of sheeting Brian had wrapped around her palms, planning her next move as she did.

Brian cried out, nearly surfacing to consciousness when she had to move his arm. Joy felt tears well up in her eyes again at the thought of how much pain he must be in and of what such a severe break might mean to his career. Carefully, she wrapped the magazine around his arm and wrist, lashing it in place with the strips of sheeting to stabilize the break.

Please let it heal okay, she prayed as she rolled him to his back and lay the splinted arm across his chest. Then it was only natural to cradle his head in her lap. Differences to the contrary, she loved him more than life and would gladly give hers for him. She just couldn't live the life he wanted.

"Let him be okay, Lord. Please. Let him be okay."

Brian opened his eyes then and frowned up at her. "You...never cry," he said, wonderingly.

"I'm not crying." She sniffled. "There's just rock dust in my eyes." But of course she *was* crying. In fact, she couldn't seem to stop. Putting her hand on the splinted arm she said, "You broke your arm. Don't move it, Bri. Okay?"

He nodded and closed his eyes. Running her fingers through his hair seemed to soothe him, so she gave into the need to touch him. Somehow that tangible connection gave her faith that he would recover. The kids never moved from their vigil on the cliff, either. They just kept watch over Brian the way she did. Praying. Thinking. Praying some more.

She wondered if the collapse had looked any different to the children. No matter how many times she reconstructed it in her mind, Joy still couldn't think of a single warning they'd had of impending disaster. But even knowing there'd been no warning, she still felt guilty. If he hadn't been so worried about having upset her—if he hadn't been trying to get to her lifeline—he might have had time to get out of the way. All he'd needed was a second to grip his own rope and swing away from the collapse.

Some time later the telltale thwop-thwop of a helicopter echoed into the canyon. It had seemed like forever but she knew it hadn't been even one hour. They might have been in the middle of nowhere on foot, but by air help had always been relatively close. She thanked God for that now.

The chopper flew in from the east and hovered for a few seconds. Joy protected Brian's face from the blowing dust and got a salute from the spotter. As the pilot rotated to fly off toward the meadow, she realized she knew and had worked with both men before. That relaxed her a bit because she knew them to be accomplished professionals. After they surveyed the situation, the chopper rotated toward the meadow and landed there. Quickly and efficiently they rappelled down using friction equipment, not Brian's over-under system that had worried her so much.

Brian woke again as they moved him into the basket. He was mentally alert but in a lot of pain as the ascent began. The pilot helped her scale the cliff and then she limped beside them as they carried Brian to the chopper. He also explained that they hadn't been sent in a bigger bird because it was thought there were only two adults to be rescued. Consequently, there was no room for all the children and her. Joy suggested Dan go with Brian since he needed a hospital. She volunteered to wait for the second chopper with the children. Together she and the pilot decided Brian would be better off in a Syracuse hospital, so the plan was to fly directly there.

Then, as the men went for Dan, Joy climbed aboard, steeling herself to say goodbye. It was what she'd wanted all along—to have him out of her life—and now that it was here, she felt as if her heart was being torn out.

"I'm staying here with the kids," she told him, hating the waver in her voice. "Dan's going with you to Syracuse."

"But you're afraid out here. Leave one of the rescue team and come with me."

It was a measure of how far she'd sunk that she was relieved he'd read fear into the waver of her voice and not the anguish this ending was costing her. "The kids are upset. They don't need a stranger right now." She pushed the hair off his forehead. "I don't think I've ever seen you so dirty, but don't worry, some pretty nurse will be giving you a sponge bath in no time." She forced herself to smile even though she had to blink to fight tears. Touching him had been another in a series of mistakes. "You take care, Bri. And I'll see to the kids. We won't be here long. There's another bird in the air on its way to get us right now."

"I'm sorry," he whispered to her just as they arrived with Dan. "I ruined everything on that ledge. I didn't mean—"

"Sh-sh." She kissed him on the forehead and added that to the list of mistakes she couldn't seem to stop making. "I know you didn't mean to hurt me. Just worry about getting better. There are lots more kids out there who need you."

He swallowed and a tear ran from his eye down the side of his face. She pretended not to notice. "I love you," he protested.

"I love you, too," she admitted and smiled sadly. The pressure behind her eyes increased threateningly. She bit her lip and blinked. She wouldn't cry. She wouldn't! "It's no one's fault."

The chopper engines whined. "We're ready to go, Joy," the pilot shouted as he put on his earphones.

She parted with the words she'd used all those years ago, only this time they were spoken with regret, not anger. "Goodbye, Bri. I'll see you around." She pivoted and jumped to the ground. She bent low and limped away to join the five children standing huddled at the edge of the meadow.

One foot in front of the other, she chanted as each step carried her away from Brian.

Joy turned as the chopper lifted and her body lost its will to stand. She plunked down into the meadow. She had no idea that she was crying until Candy tried drying her tears with the edge of her jacket. Then Adam

was there patting her on the shoulder and Mike was assuring her that Brian was tough and he'd be fine. Candy
said they'd all see him real soon. Kevin sat down and
just took her hand and Chad handed her the last of the
torn-up sheet to use as a hanky.

She knew she was supposed to be fulfilling all these
roles for them and she tried desperately to stop, but all
she could do was cry harder. Wracking sobs erupted and
she rocked—five worried children looking on in horror
as their stalwart super-woman fell apart before their
eyes. And still she cried.

Brian woke from a short nap in his room in a Syracuse hospital. There was still no decision yet on what
they'd do with his wrist. He and the orthopedist were
waiting for test results. He knew he should be worried
to death about the breaks. They were severe and his
career depended on how bad the MRI looked. But he
couldn't muster one scrap of concern. He knew the top
hand-and-wrist man in the country personally—had
lunch with Lee at least twice a month. If it was bad, he'd
told the orthopedist to stabilize it and ship him home.

He'd prayed and that was what felt right. The Lord was
in charge of his life from now on. Because he'd loused it
up good and proper trying to plan it out on his own.

All he could think about at that point was the
broken look on Joy's face as she'd backed away from
him on the ledge and then her expression when she'd
said goodbye in the chopper. He couldn't get past it.
He'd hurt her so badly and now that he thought about
it, she'd been saying goodbye.

Not goodbye—she'd be by to see him as soon as she could. That would have meant she'd realized she couldn't live without him, no matter that he wasn't her idea of Prince Charming.

And it hadn't been goodbye and they'd never see each other again. That would have been be bad enough, but at least it would mean she cared enough that seeing him would be painful. That might give him a fighting chance.

But she hadn't said that.

Her goodbye meant she'd given up on him—on them. That she'd tried and couldn't even contemplate a life with him and what she called his dark-ages ideas. That she didn't care enough to avoid him.

"Where in the Bible did it ever say women can't work outside the home?" he muttered, repeating the question Joy had asked on the cliff.

"Nowhere I ever saw," his nurse quipped as she hustled into the room. "Seems to me, back when the Bible was written, women had such a full day with household chores there wasn't time or energy left for anything. We're no busier now. Just differently. I probably have more time with my kids than my mother did. I pay someone to clean, and I either work night shift while they sleep and sleep while they're in school, or day shift and leave work before they get home from school."

Brian stared at the fortysomething woman. "What's your husband do?"

She chuckled and looked at her watch. "Right now I'd say my husband's reading your MRI."

Her husband was the orthopedist? And she had a career. But it wasn't a dangerous one like Joy's, he reminded himself. And she had kids because she wanted them. He wasn't convinced Joy did.

"Your rescue sure caused a media stir around here. Your family called while you were asleep to say they were on their way. They were up at Piseco and hadn't known you were hurt until your friend the pilot told them. The rescue is the lead story on the national news. They'll probably show footage of the landing of the helicopter at Piseco." She pointed to the TV hanging on the other side of the small room. "You want to watch?"

A chance to see for himself that Joy and the kids got out safely? He nodded, not trusting his voice as emotions rose up to choke him.

Six days.

It had only been six days. They rushed across his mind's eye. Each day had held so much living. So much discovery. So much closeness.

Now he was alone again. And in so much pain.

The TV picture bloomed on just as the blades of a helicopter slowed to a stop. Adam and Joy were the first out, then Chad and Kevin tumbled out behind her. Adam lifted Candy to the ground and the rescue worker helped Mike jump down. An announcer recited their identities as they turned toward the camera. Then they were mobbed. Anna Lovell and Jim ran to meet Joy and engulf her in their embrace. The same scene happened around each of the children. Family. Tears. Hugs and kisses.

Meanwhile, cameras flashed as the kids and Joy, families in tow, entered a building. The news anchor said all the children had checked out well and then he droned on with facts about Joy's career and Brian's. There was also some speculation that though Joy appeared to have been injured only slightly in the crash, the injuries Brian suffered on the cliff were so severe he might never operate again.

"Don't you pay that any attention. It has to be sensational to grab public attention these days and that's the name of their game," the nurse said.

"Thanks, but I'm not too worried," Brian said.

"Maybe you should be, doctor," a man who was clearly a doctor himself said as he came into the room. "It's bad. I might have fused the wrist and been done with it if I didn't know you're a surgeon. I've already called that friend of yours and he has other ideas. So I'm going to do what you suggested earlier. I'll set the upper ulna break and stabilize the lower comminuted fracture. I'm not embarrassed to say I'm not in his league and I'd do you a great disservice trying to tackle this kind of reconstruction."

Brian felt suddenly rudderless. He was tempted to ask how many pieces there were to the fracture but that wasn't his problem. The pain of losing any chance with Joy was beginning to numb everything else. "So how do I go about getting out of here and getting home?"

"Joy has a plane en route for us," his brother Greg said from behind the orthopedist. Greg stepped around the doctor and smiled. He moved toward the bed and carefully hugged Brian. "You were always such an overachiever. Get in a plane crash and you rescue everyone. Mom and Dad are out there trying to satisfy the reporters clamoring to hear all about brave Doctor Brian Peterson."

Brian's spirit brightened but not because his family was there. If Joy was flying him home, maybe she'd changed her mind. Maybe she hadn't given up on them. "We're flying home with Joy?"

Greg stared at him, then frowned. "No," he said carefully. "She's going home with Jim and Anna. She sent a jet here to Syracuse for us."

He knew his face fell and Brian didn't care. "Oh."

"You're disappointed."

He stared at his brother. His pastor. He'd hidden his feelings from his family and himself for years. No more. "I'm in love with her. I have been for years. And now I've lost her. Wouldn't you be disappointed?"

Chapter Sixteen

"Now there's a hangdog look if ever there was one," Joy heard her Uncle George say from behind her. She looked up and caught his eyes watching her reflection in the tinted window.

She looked away from her study of the scenery outside her office window and spun her desk chair back toward him and the pile of papers covering her desk. "Morning, Uncle George. I was just thinking." Even she heard the sigh in her voice.

"Dangerous stuff, deciding on the fate of the world before coffee. Or were you trying to decide whether you should just shred all this—" he gestured to the untidy pile of papers on her desk "—or handle it?" She noticed the overburdened coffee caddy in his hand. He chuckled. "Of course handling it without coffee and blueberry muffins could be dangerous, too."

She stared at the coffee cups numbly. It was a good thing it was his day to pick it up at the coffee shop or they'd both be caffeine-starved. She'd arrived at the field half an hour ago with her brain still not firing on all cylinders. She'd had another restless night, which wasn't unusual since her sojourn in the Adirondack Forest Preserve.

Shaking off the funk of days past—or at least trying to—she reached out for the coffee. "Oh, bless you. No wonder you're my favorite uncle. Maybe this will clear the cobwebs away."

"Two creams, no sugar. Just like always."

She smiled sadly and accepted the take-out cup across her desk. She took a sip while he set a muffin in front of her. "Um. And I wasn't contemplating the fate of the world or the paperwork. Just my life," Joy admitted, needing some advice or at least a sounding board. Uncle George had been hers since her teens.

"You ain't been yourself since you got back last week."

"No. I haven't been myself." Joy stared down at her hand. The blisters from the crutch and the trek up the mountain were nearly healed. She broke a piece off her muffin and catalogued the rest of her Adirondack injuries. Her shoulder was fine. Her ankle? Not so fine but getting there. Her heart…

"Am I wrong to want to be me?" she blurted. "What I'm wondering is if wanting to be who I am is worth losing a chance to have more in my life. Especially because I'd lose so much of what I have now."

Uncle George blinked and his face screwed up in confusion. "Say what?"

Maybe that didn't make much sense without some important information. "It's Brian. I love him. Still. Again. And he loves me, too."

"Last I heard love isn't supposed to make you miserable and, toots, you've been miserable since you got back. Same old problem?"

She nodded. "He thinks I can't be a pilot *and* be a wife and mother. I know it wouldn't be easy but it wouldn't be impossible."

"And?" he urged.

"And nothing." She smacked her hand on her desk. "I don't see why I should have to give up Agape Air and stay home just to win him. You know I like nice things and that I have a nice place. I don't expect to hang a plasma screen on the hangar wall, stick a couch in front of it and call it home for my husband and kids. But I'd be bored to tears with nothing but home to think about. I'm just not good with committees and that sort of thing. It'd be no different than in high school. They'd start acting all catty, my head would explode and I'd tell them exactly what I thought of them. And then Brian's career would suffer or at the very least his relationships with his colleagues would."

"You've negotiated contracts with some pretty arrogant men who run international companies and you haven't unloaded on them. You're not the same girl you were at seventeen. You've grown into a woman with a woman's control—a pilot's control. I think you could handle a bunch of committee ladies. I can't help feel you're sellin' yourself short, toots. And Brian, right along with you. Have you ever sat down and told him all this? Have you tried to talk it out?"

"Of course I did! I told him I couldn't change—"

Uncle George raised his hand palm up stopping her

midthought. "Did you tell him how you plan to stay on here and still handle having and raising little ones? Or did you get all huffy?" He used his upraised hand again, stopping her reply. "Don't answer me. It isn't for me to know. Just you answer truthfully in your heart. Breaking things off with him back when you were so young wasn't a mistake, but you're both older and you've both got some experience with life under your belts. Think about it."

Joy didn't even notice him shuffling out as she turned away from her desk and looked out at all she and Uncle George had built. She thought back over every conversation she and Brian had had and admitted that they'd never really talked about either of their expectations of marriage this time. And that was her fault. She'd been too busy guarding her heart to find out if he'd changed his vision. And she honestly had to wonder if Brian even knew she wanted children at all.

Was that what he'd been trying to say on the cliff? That he thought it was a shame she'd decided to forego having children in favor of her career because she'd be a good mother? Or had he meant it the way it sounded— that he didn't think she could have both? She didn't know. And she'd been too leery of him to talk about her dreams because once before he hadn't honored them. And so she'd never told him she wanted marriage and motherhood to be in her future.

The memory of the tears she'd seen in his eyes rose up to haunt her. This wasn't just about her. They were both hurting. And that was just wrong. Especially if it was needless suffering. She pushed herself to her feet.

If she and Brian had to lose each other, it was time to make sure they each knew why.

Joy nearly turned back several times on her way to the hospital, but she pulled into the parking garage, her heart pounding with anticipation of seeing him again and trepidation for the same reason.

She knew Brian had been transferred to the rehab floor after his surgery but only because her brother made sure she knew it. Everyone kept asking her how he was doing, then looked at her askance when she said she hadn't had time to go see him. She'd had the time; what she hadn't had was the courage.

Moving slowly toward his room, she entered the elevator and hit the button for the sixth floor. All too soon the elevator stopped and it was either step off or retreat. Joy had no problem with regrouping, but to retreat was another thing altogether. The only thing worse, she knew, would be surrender. So she approached his room determined to state her case and let him choose.

The room was decorated in pastel colors in the cutesy-country theme so many hospitals thought made the patients feel at home. It was brightened by a profusion of flowers covering every surface, but if they were suppose to cover the antiseptic hospital smell they failed. She hated that he'd wound up here fighting for his career when all she'd had to do was file insurance claims and await the result of an FAA inquiry into the crash.

Then she saw him and seriously worried that she would not be strong enough to walk away again no matter what. Brian sat across the room in a chair near the windows. He looked a little pale and as if he might be in pain. He wore a faraway, sad expression and there were lines of strain around his eyes. Though there was a book in his lap, he wasn't reading it but was staring at the opposite wall of the little window alcove where he sat.

"Hi, Bri, how is it going?" she asked, trying for a casual greeting when she felt anything but casual. What she felt was desperate for even this glimpse of him. Her stomach churned, her voice felt weak and she was afraid it sounded just as unsubstantial.

Bright sunlight streamed in and sparkled in his golden hair, but the brilliance that came into his dark eyes when he saw her put the sunlight to shame. The strain disappeared and the pain she'd thought she'd seen was a forgotten figment of her imagination in a milli-second.

"Joy! You came," he said, and as he put aside the book she realized now that it was his much-used Bible. "I'd just about given up hope."

There was no other chair by the windows, giving Joy a choice of where to sit. She could push the chair by the bed nearer to him, and almost did. But then she remembered the insects that had buzzed too near the flames of their campfire. Her wings were already singed. She'd gone close enough.

"I'm sorry I didn't get here before this," Joy told him as she perched on the bottom of the bed while memorizing his face for later. "I'd give you the same excuse I've given everyone else but you'd know I wasn't too busy catching up at work."

"What made you finally come?" he asked, his tone hesitant and achingly hopeful, his gaze fixed on her face.

She felt a sad smile tug at her lips. "Besides missing you? I'm here because I got to thinking that when we were sitting on the ledge I didn't give you a chance to explain what you meant and I'm sorry. You got hurt because I refused to listen. You didn't notice you were in danger because you were distracted by our argument."

Brian closed his eyes for a second and touched his now crinkled forehead. Then he looked up and drew her gaze as no man ever had. "I got hurt because a cliff wall that had been standing there for thousands of years suddenly let go. And if you hadn't moved when you did, we both could have been killed. So no one's to blame. Okay?"

She looked at his casted arm and shook her head. "Only after you tell me you're going to be all right."

"Lee says I'll be fine after he and his physical therapist torture me for several months." He shrugged, but it wasn't quite the careless gesture she thought he meant it to be. "I was overdue for a vacation anyway," he went on. "The intense stuff will be over at the end of the week and I'll go home. Probably to Greg's house, although with his tribe I don't see it being particularly restful."

Relieved, she breathed easily for the first time since moving the rock and seeing his damaged wrist. "Praise God. I don't think I ever prayed harder than I have this week."

He grinned. "I'm flattered considering lightning shot a plane out from under you two weeks ago."

She smiled. "We weren't in the damaged plane all

that long. I hardly had a chance to do more than call out to Him for wisdom and mercy."

"It seemed like forever," Brian said and winced. "That was one whale of a first flight."

Did he mean—? "Oh, no. Bri, that was your first time in an airplane?" She remembered with fondness his old, beat-up Oldsmobile. "That's right. You used to drive back and forth from college. I'm so sorry. It really is a safe way to travel."

Brian chuckled. "I figure since lightning never strikes twice in the same place, I have a sixty-year pass on plane crashes. You, too."

They'd gotten entirely off subject. And much as she enjoyed talking to Brian about nothing at all, she had to get this settled. The trouble was, Joy was pretty sure she hadn't been this nervous taking any of her piloting tests. Not even on her first solo flight at sixteen had she been this terrified. Maybe because more than her future hung in the balance. This was about her heart and her happiness—Brian's, too. And there could be no future for them if they didn't talk.

"All this talk of planes reminds me of why I came to see you." She took a deep breath and willed herself to look into his eyes as she asked, "What did you mean about me being wasted as a pilot?"

His deep chocolate eyes looked uncertain. Brian was never uncertain. She hated that she had done this to him.

"I won't blow up," she promised. Joy was determined this time to let him say whatever he needed to say no matter how much it hurt—no matter how much she wanted to run from it. She had to know if they had a chance or at least the full reason why they didn't. "If we don't talk this out, it'll haunt us. Our families are close. If we can't work this out the two of us are doomed to have every family occasion rip the scab off the wounds or we'll have to keep avoiding each other. I don't know about you, but I'm sick of turning your brother down every time he asks me to one of his kids' birthday parties."

"Me, too." Brian's reply was more of a sigh. Then he pursed his lips, pausing for a long moment. It was clear he was as worried about his answer as she was. "I meant that Agape Air has been like your child. And it's fulfilled you, but that it's a shame you don't want kids because you'd be a great mother."

She tilted her head and frowned. "Bri, where did you get the idea I don't want kids? I just don't see why I can't do both and as far as I know, you don't see how I can."

Brian opened his mouth but was interrupted by the click of high heels on the linoleum. They both looked toward the door.

"Well, there you are, Brian Peterson," a gorgeous woman called out as she floated into the room on three inch heels. Her pink silk suit was the perfect foil for her creamy complexion and blue-black hair.

Snow White meets the new millennium, Joy thought, sourly. But though Joy wanted to hate the perfect creature who'd just entered, Snow's sweet smile wouldn't let her.

"I was here earlier," the tiny woman continued on, "and the lioness at the gate told me you were off to therapy. But she wouldn't tell me where exactly. She said you couldn't be interrupted. I wanted to be your

cheer—" Miss S. White's eyes met Joy's, widening in
surprise. "Oh, I'm so sorry. I didn't see you sitting
there." She put her perfectly manicured hand out and
Joy shook it, conscious of her own blister-roughened
palms and her unisex uniform.

"Joy Lovell," she said, trying not to show how inad-
equate she felt and how unused she was to feeling that
way.

"How *are* you? You were Brian's pilot. I'm Linda
Haversham. Brian's partner is my husband. I'm in awe
of what you do but I can't imagine doing a job that
scares me silly." She giggled. "Though my kids terrify
me on a daily basis."

Joy found herself smiling genuinely but before she
could respond to the joke, Linda Haversham went on. "I
hope you don't mind if I interrupt for a moment. I need
to talk to Brian about something Memorial's ladies auxiliary needs him to do. We all decided on it at a dinner party
last night but of course, Brian, you couldn't be there."

Joy waved her on, frustrated with the woman's
timing. She tuned out most of the conversation but she
got the gist of it. She looked at sweet, warm and perfect Linda "Snow White" Haversham and saw cold
reality.

*This is what Brian needs in a wife. This kind of
woman. The dinner party kind. The committee kind.
The kind of woman I not only can't be, but won't be.*

The differences between her and Brian were about
more than children and day care. It was about living in
two different worlds. Brian deserved the right woman
at his side. One who liked his world. If Joy let him, she

knew by the look she'd seen leap to Brian's eyes when she'd walked in earlier that he'd settle for her. Joy couldn't do that to him or herself. Because settling and being settled for would destroy them both eventually.

So as Linda and Brian finalized plans for some bachelor-auction fund-raiser, Joy, tears glistening in her eyes, slipped from the room and from Brian's life. And she'd never felt so alone in her life.

Brian glanced toward Joy to share a private smile while categorically refusing to take part in Linda's fund-raiser. The grin froze on his lips and the words lodged in his throat. Joy was gone.

Linda followed his gaze to the empty place where Joy had been perched. "Why do I get the feeling I couldn't have picked a worse time to come in here?"

"It's par for the course with Joy and me. We were out in the middle of nowhere for six days and didn't manage to get things settled between us."

"Things. What things? Come on. Tell Mama Linda what this is all about."

"It's nothing. Really. Listen, I'm really tired."

"In other words, 'go away, I'd rather sulk on my own.'"

He winced but nodded.

Linda made an entirely female sound of disapproval. "I hate it when men go all silent and broody. You saved my son's life two years ago and I won't let you be miserable. I'm not leaving, so you may as well cooperate, and let me help you understand her sudden disappearance. Answer a question for me. Am I right in assuming she is the reason you won't do the auction this year?"

Brian nodded absently, trying to figure out what had sent Joy fleeing from his room.

"Do you think she was jealous because I asked you to be in the auction?"

"I said I wouldn't—besides Joy isn't the jealous type," he responded immediately. "She's the most self-assured woman I've ever met."

He felt a helpless grin tug at his lips remembering her near tirade in the cave. *I fly over this. I rescue people from this. I don't sleep in it. And I sure don't eat cute little bunnies for dinner. I just want to go home.* That hadn't been all of it but it was a good cross section. So, okay. She had her fears just like they all did. He knew she was even more afraid of being hurt again. But she'd come to see him and he'd thought she'd settled down to talk things out. "She'd come to talk. So what changed?" Brian wondered aloud.

"I did," Linda put in. "So what about me would spook a tall, gorgeous blonde with her own million-dollar business? I'm married, so that couldn't be it. Not my looks. As I said, she's gorgeous and it didn't take an expert makeup job to make her look like that."

Brian frowned. He thought about Joy's expression when Linda had walked in. It wasn't that. She'd only looked bemused and a bit annoyed to have been interrupted. "No. She never cared about that sort of thing. We were stuck out there for six days and she didn't once complain about her hair, her dirty clothes or anything. Except for wishing for a shower, which even the kids and I wanted."

The next time he'd glanced at Joy, Linda was into her

sales pitch and Joy was gone. He was stumped. "Do me a favor. Find Lee. Or Rick. I want out of here."

"Ah, you're going after her." Linda smiled. "The direct approach. I like that, so I'll help you. 'Faint heart ne'er won fair lady.' I'll have you sprung in an hour."

Chapter Seventeen

Agape Air buzzed with activity. All around Brian as he walked toward the office, men and women rushed hither and yon on missions of what looked like great importance. The last time he'd been there his whole attention had been on his young patient. He'd obviously missed a lot.

Brian stopped and looked around, wanting to get a feel for Joy's world. A mechanic and a pilot, both dressed in the blue and khaki uniform he was used to seeing Joy wear, conferred over an engine. A small sky-blue-and-white jet sporting the Agape Air logo took off. A business man who carried himself like a corporate tiger paced and checked his watch. Then a young woman approached him and pointed him toward a sparkling commuter jet that looked as if it had just rolled off the assembly line. It too sported the Agape cloud and wings. Mr. Businessman's scowl changed to a look of delight.

There was so much going on that Brian wondered if

coming here had been a mistake. He'd hate to have yet another important talk cut short. Feeling a little unsure of himself, Brian looked back at Linda Haversham where she sat waiting for him in her car. She made a shooing motion urging him inside the office and mouthed, "Go."

He knew she was right, and went.

The walls were the colors of the planes, light blue with bold slashes of white, a wide counter separated a large office area from an empty waiting lounge. George Brady sat at a stainless steel desk in the area behind the counter, growling at someone on the phone.

Brian looked at the scheduling board and took it in, feeling a faint shock. He'd known Joy had expanded the company but he'd had no idea Agape's fleet of small planes was so large or that she employed so many people. His head spun. How could he compete with Agape Air and Joy's central position in the company? He'd been a fool to have ever thought she should or could give this up. This was what made Joy who she was.

The woman he loved.

Brady looked up when the bell over the door tinkled. The old man shot a killing glance Brian's way. "Just you stay available for the return flight or Joy's going to want to know why," he said to the person on the other end of the line. Then he listened for a moment. "I know but that bigwig from LaFleur was mighty angry till she placated him with this solution." Again he waited for a response. "Yeah, he'll be aboard any minute." George chuckled. "No, I wouldn't want to cross Joy today, either. She's like a bear with a sore paw."

"And here's the thorn," he grumbled, glaring at Brian as he set down the phone.

Brian sighed. This whole idea was starting to feel like a bad idea. His legs were shaky and the sling holding his casted arm hung around his neck like a millstone. His wrist ached really badly, too. "What I'd like to know is why I'm the problem and not the solution," he replied.

George's gaze sharpened even though he leaned back in his chair and crossed his arms lazily. "You should've been. Do you really want to know why you're the problem instead?"

"I checked myself out of rehab to come here. My doctors were still screaming when I got in the car. What do you think? I don't have a clue what happened. Joy and I had just started talking when a friend stopped by. Before we knew it, Joy was gone."

"Humph. She came back here. Been crying. All red-eyed." George shook his head jerkily. "Never saw her like that." Again he glared at Brian.

At a loss, Brian felt his heart squeeze. Joy never cried. But then those fuzzy memories after the cliff collapsed on him came back flooding back. She'd cried then. Over him. "What did she say when she came back?" he insisted on knowing.

"That she was going to save you from yourself. We talked some, then she went in her office and cried some more. Then she got down to business clearin' her desk like a tornado cuttin' through a trailer park. She's on the phone right now with the FAA about something she didn't like in Pittsburgh yesterday to do with airport security. They just got back to her on it."

Brian glanced at the only lit phone line, anxious to talk to Joy. But then something occurred to him. George Brady might be able to unravel this quicker than he could. "What exactly is Joy saving me from?"

"Appears your visitor is perfect for you."

Brian blinked in surprise and laid his throbbing wrist on the counter. "Joy knows Linda is only a friend. Linda even introduced herself as my partner's wife," he explained.

Joy's Uncle George shook his head. "She means you need her *kind* of woman. Joy has it in her head that she can't deal with most women like your friend. I think it's more that she doesn't want to deal with them and so she's afraid she'd mess it up. Accidentally on purpose if you get my drift. She thinks she'd make you miserable, you'd lose your friends and your professional connections. I had her talked around all this and a few other things earlier in the morning so she went to see you but then seeing…" George screwed up his face in an exaggerated grimace. "'Snow White,' she called her, convinced Joy otherwise."

Brian thought back. They'd been talking about the ladies auxiliary. "I never said I expect Joy to join charity committees."

"Ya did years ago," George reminded him.

Yes, he had. He'd had Joy's role in his life well-defined. He'd acted like an arrogant child instead of the adult he saw himself as. This was starting to make sense. "And I never told her otherwise. Just the way Joy told me she didn't want kids—years ago. Now she says she does."

George shook his head. "I think she meant later. She never said never all those years ago."

Brian nodded and shifted to lean on the counter with his good arm, thinking he wasn't as ready to be out and about as he'd thought. "She'd only just straightened that out when my friend came in. We never got into how she planned to have kids and run this place but—"

Brady lost his relaxed posture and shuffled over to the counter. "There's a small office connected to hers. When I didn't want it, she said if the Lord sent the right man her way, maybe she'd get to use it as a playroom and nursery. But I don't see you talking Joy around to you being that man. She thinks you'll settle for her and resent her and your life later on. She's on a crusade to save you from yourself. Nothing's harder to get by than Joy on a crusade."

Brian nearly groaned. Instead he glanced down at the phone, wanting desperately to see Joy. The line was still lit and he was feeling past tired all the way to exhaustion. Maybe the Lord was telling him something—like that he ought to take the time to think before he saw her. The thought gave him pause. He needed to think this time before he acted. He'd talked to George and got a lot of questions answered so he had to wonder what kind of insight talking to her brother and his wife and Anna Lovell would give him. Something flowered to life in him and he recognized it as hope.

"Do me a favor, George. Don't tell her I was here. I'm going to fix this. I don't know how yet, but I'll do it. I have to."

* * *

When a knock sounded at her door, Joy looked around her living room—a reflex for someone prone to leaving things a bit undone. But the place was neat, though she couldn't say when she'd straightened things. Life, she realized, could be lived on autopilot but it was about as much of a challenge as flying that way.

She'd agreed to a visit from her brother Jim's mother-in-law. Joy didn't know exactly what kind of family relationship she had to her brother's mother-in-law but it was a bond of family that Joy felt to Meg Taggert Alton nonetheless. Meg was still considered a local icon even though she only lived half the year at Laurel Glen, the horse farm where she'd been raised and had lived many of her adult years. The farm shared a border with Joy's much smaller property. Curious about the purpose of the visit, Joy went down to let her elegant, fiftysomething neighbor in, then served them both tea at the dinette table.

In her typical no-nonsense style, Meg got down to the purpose of her visit as soon as she'd sweetened her tea. "I'm hoping you'll agree to help us with something," she said, her platinum hair gleaming in the sunlight that streamed in Joy's fairy-tale windows. "I've gotten interested in Angel Flight. Your brother mentioned you fly for them quite a bit as do most of your pilots. I've decided to host a benefit for the organization at Laurel Glen. I'm hoping you'll help out."

It wasn't really Joy's thing, but Angel Flight was her pet charity. "What can I do?"

"We're going to host a dinner party and silent auction at Laurel Glen next Saturday evening. With all the stories following the crash I started thinking what a big asset you could be to the night."

Now Joy understood. Meg wanted to be able to publicize a donation from Agape for the auction. "How about we kick in a round-trip flight on our newest corporate jet to a vacation destination?"

Meg was clearly taken aback for a moment. Her sapphire eyes widened, then she tilted her head, giving Joy a long assessing look. "That wasn't exactly what I had in mind, although it would certainly help. I thought you might come to the dinner."

"Next Saturday?"

"I am sorry this is so last-minute but Jim mentioned you'd gone back to work. He was sure you were up to an evening out. I'd hoped you would consider using your recent celebrity to Angel Flight's advantage now that you're feeling better."

Joy set her cup down just a bit too hard. This wasn't what she'd expected. "I don't understand."

"We hoped you would circulate among the guests and let them ask you questions about your Angel Flight experiences. Perhaps about the rescue. And, of course, chat up donations. That sort of thing."

The idea made Joy uncomfortable and she was so drained emotionally over Brian that she just didn't have the energy to tackle something so out of her usual range. "I've never done anything like that. I'm not even sure I could."

"Well, of course you could." Meg looked at her, surprise written on her youthful features. "You deal with corporate executives all the time. You told me that yourself. What's the difference? You're just getting money out of the guests for a worthy charity instead of out of a business associate for a service. And they'd still be getting something for their money. We've put together some interesting packages for them to bid on. Lavender Hill donated riding lessons. My brother, Ross, offered a child's birthday party at Laurel Glen complete with pony rides, and his wife Amelia offered to take pictures of all the little ones. A local gym offered a year's membership. There are more, of course. I'll familiarize you with what's being offered later in the week but you get the idea. Oh, say you will. You won't be the only one circulating, but your being involved would be such a boost."

Jim had often said no one could say no to his mother-in-law and now Joy understood. She sighed. "Oh, okay. I don't have anything better to do with my Saturday night."

Meg smiled and left not long after. Joy wished she understood why the woman looked so relieved and excited. It wasn't as if Laurel Glen didn't host charity functions all the time. She couldn't imagine them thinking they needed her presence to make it a success.

Brian picked up the phone on the first ring. He'd been waiting to hear from Meg Alton. He was more than a little nervous putting such an important plan in the hands of a virtual stranger, even if that stranger was Jim Lovell's mother-in-law. "It's all set," a voice on the other end called out in answer to his greeting.

"Mrs. Alton?"

She laughed gleefully. "Sorry, I'm just so excited at

how this is all coming together." Brian heard the motor start. "I've just left her. She's completely on board though I think she's a bit overwhelmed by the idea. Now all you have to do is deliver a good portion of the guests to this last-minute fund-raiser. Leave the rest up to Crystal and me. I have plenty of local arms to twist for contributions. I've got to go, dear. I hate to drive and talk on the phone. I'll be in touch about timing. Take care now, dear, and do those exercises Jim says you need to do."

Brian stared at the suddenly dead phone. When he'd asked Jim for help, he hadn't realized Jim's mother-in-law was a gleefully unrepentant matchmaker. He grinned. Thanks to her it looked as if this plan just might come together better than he'd dared hope.

Chapter Eighteen

Joy drove under the iron entrance arch of Laurel Glen Horse Farm hardly noticing the picture-perfect setting of crisscrossing white fences, rolling green hills, quaint stone and brick stables or its famous octagonal barn. She knew why this view wound up in every pictorial done of rural Chester County, Pennsylvania, but today she didn't care. This was not her usual reason for being here.

This evening, as the sun sank behind the distant tree covered hills, the tranquil scene did nothing to calm Joy's jangled nerves. Laurel House loomed larger than ever on the hill overlooking the horse farm and for the first time she thought it looked a bit forbidding.

She could have said no to this dinner party, of course, but something had told her she needed to do it. What had she been thinking? she asked herself now. She drove on and once again she demanded to know what she was afraid of. But it did no good. Her stomach muscles had knotted to the point of nausea, so before she disgraced herself she turned to the one thing she knew would help. The one *person*. She turned her mind and heart to prayer knowing it would do a lot more than any of her self-directed pep talks had.

So, by the time she'd driven the mile in from the main road, her thoughts were less scattered and her nausea was all but gone. As she'd been told, she stopped at the foot of Laurel House's stone steps and turned her car over to a waiting valet.

She turned and faced the house. Rather than find a forbidding and imposing set of stone steps, some clever designer had softened the hard-scape. The house was encircled by three terraces and the steps between each level were randomly offset. The arrangement invited the visitor to stop and enjoy the profusion of potted plants on each of the terraces and the wonderful scenery beyond. At the second level Joy did just that, and God's beauty, placed in the hands of a family of believers, nearly finished the job her prayer had begun.

Calmer than she'd been in days, Joy turned away from the perfection of the view and began the last part of her ascent. Meg Alton met her there, her ready smile welcoming as always. She was lovely in an ice-blue long skirt and a beaded top. Her striking platinum hair, always so surprising with her dark eyebrows, was swept up on top of her head completing a look of cool sophistication. Joy knew the impression didn't reflect the older woman's warm personality at all. She found a bit more confidence, seeing from the formality of Meg's attire, that her own sleeveless Chinese-inspired dress would fit in just fine.

"You look beautiful tonight, dear," Meg said, leading the way into the lovely foyer of Laurel House. "That's such a wonderful shade of teal." She turned to Joy and took her hands, her own cool and a little jittery. "Did you get time to look over the packages for the auctions?"

Joy nodded and handed her shawl to a man stationed near the sweeping staircase. "I was surprised by the list. You certainly beat the bushes for contributions," she told Meg.

"A little too well, I'm afraid. Ross has been teasing me, as only a brother can, about one package I put together." Meg grimaced. "And though I hate to admit it, he may be right. How on earth are we going to approach any woman and sell her a makeover? 'Pardon me, dear, but you just don't look your best. Perhaps you'd like to bid on this makeover.' I'm completely out of practice I'm afraid. It's a disaster."

Joy laughed. "And if a man bought it for his wife he'd be implying she needs help with her appearance. Talk about World War Three on a small scale." Yet when she'd heard about the package she'd thought of her sister-in-law, who could use a day of pampering but who already had a wonderful sense of style. Since giving birth to Emmy, she doubted Crystal had had an hour just to herself with no responsibilities to worry about.

"I have an idea," she told Meg as they moved together into a room full of milling guests. "With tomorrow being Mother's Day what if we don't call it a makeover, but a Mother's Day gift? An afternoon of pampering topped off with a free shopping expedition and fashion tips from a local designer."

Meg clapped her hands together. "Oh, thank you, thank you. I knew you'd be really wonderful at this. After all, you're an accomplished businesswoman—what's a little silent auction to someone with so much experience in negotiating and public relations?"

It was a lightbulb moment for Joy. She looked around the dazzling room. Of course she could do this. Why had she doubted herself? She grinned, feeling better than she had in weeks. Still, she sensed there was more significance to the moment than she had time to discover right then. She had a job to do. "Suppose I see what I can do about getting a bidding war going between all the new fathers in the neighborhood," Joy suggested. "For instance, I see your nephew Cole over there with CJ. She could certainly use a little pampering. I doubt she gets much downtime between her job as Laurel Glen's trainer and looking after their son."

"CJ at a spa?" Meg looked at Joy askance. "That I'd pay to see."

Joy looked away from the expression of adoration in Cole's eyes as he inclined his sable head toward CJ and bussed his tiny blond dynamo of a wife on the cheek. It was hard, she thought with a pang, to be around so many couples who were so clearly in love. But knowing CJ's reputation when it came to primping, she managed a chuckle. "Okay, CJ wasn't the best example. But Ross could give it to Amelia. Surely she could use some down time from chasing after Laurel and Rose."

"Well, yes, and my brother never skimps when it comes to Amelia."

"And considering that the school year is winding

down at Lavender Hill, Jeff Carrington could certainly indulge your niece."

Meg crossed her arms, considering the idea. "Hmm. This was a hard year for Hope, what with being pregnant with Jason and having Faith break her leg so severely on the ice."

"We should be able to get the bidding up to a nice figure. And there are sure to be other harried mothers here that neither of us even know about yet."

Joy saw her brother across the room. "And speaking of new parents, I see my inspiration right now. I'll check in and see how the rest of you are progressing."

Joy walked up behind Jim and Crystal and stepped between them. "How was Emmy when you left her?"

They turned to her, wearing identical grins. "Wrapping her sitter around her tiny finger," Crystal said. Jim's dark-haired wife was the only woman Joy had ever met she could look straight in the eye. Right now though, Crystal looked down at her watch instead and worried at her lip. "Could you keep your brother out of trouble while I call home? I just want to check on how she's doing?"

Jim grinned. "Go. You'll feel better. I'm sure Joy can keep me from arresting anyone and embarrassing you."

Joy watched Crystal for a moment as she hurried away toward the foyer, her dress a long slash of scarlet that contrasted beautifully with her long dark hair. She pulled out her cell phone as she stepped out the front door.

Joy turned her gaze on her brother, who had also followed his wife's progress across the room. Much as she loved both of them it had become difficult to be around them since she got back. They had everything she longed for and feared she would never have.

Forcing her mind to another track, Joy tapped Jim. "And that call she's making wouldn't happen to ease your mind as well, Daddy?"

"She's just so little and helpless," Jim said in his own defense, no less worried than the new mother.

"Yes, she is. And Crystal could use a break from supplying those needs 24/7. So could you pay attention here, brother mine? This event is not only your first time leaving Emmy with a sitter but it is also a *fund-raiser, capiche?"*

"I know. And I understand it's your job to rope me into spending some of my hard-earned money for your pet charity but you could give your own brother a break."

She grinned. "Ah, but you got me into this so I'm showing no mercy. But I can also make you a very popular husband. Believe me, you want to bid on the day at the spa and the boutique shopping trip. You can give it to Crystal as part of her Mother's Day gift. And good sister and aunty that I am, I promise to babysit with you, or for you, if you have to work on the day she wants to go. *If* you win it, that is."

Jim grinned. "Which means I'm not the only one you're offering this advice to this evening."

"Hey. *Fund-raiser,*" Joy reminded him with the exaggerated patience only a sister feels toward her brother. "It's my job to drive up the price. Now if you'll excuse me—"

"Wait," Jim ordered and stopped her from leaving with a hand on her arm. "You've been avoiding me since you got back. Are you okay?"

She squeezed his hand. "I'm fine."

"Joy."

"Okay," she sighed, "I'll *be* fine."

Jim looked at her with narrowed eyes. "Do I need to take Peterson apart?"

Joy felt her protective instinct rise to the surface and she didn't even think of what her instant defense would say to her brother. "You leave Brian alone. He's been through a lot. He could have lost his career, not to mention his life. You don't know what it was like on that ledge. All that rock covering him."

Her brother put his arm around her. The expression in his usually calm brown eyes was just this side of fierce. "But he didn't die and neither did you, thank the good Lord. I like Brian. Always have. But if he hurts you again, he and I are going to have a long talk."

"Brian can't help who he is anymore than I can help who I am. Leave him alone. I mean it," she warned, poking his chest.

"Okay. Okay. Just don't sell yourself short. All right?"

She stared at him but didn't have a clue what he was talking about. Still, his watchful gaze made her want to squirm. She nodded in agreement just to put an end to the subject. "I have to circulate, big brother. Don't forget to bid on that day at the spa."

Still wondering how Jim knew Brian had ever hurt her when she'd hidden her feelings behind a show of anger, Joy moved through the crowd and spotted the couple who had sold her the carriage house. They were her nearest neighbors, and relatively new parents. "Adam. Xandra," she said. "How's the baby?"

Xandra smiled broadly. "Wonderful. Luke's at home with Mark babysitting. I miss him but it's nice to be out with adults. I honestly forgot how to do more with my hair tonight than just pull it up in a ponytail. I'm trying to talk Adam into bidding on the makeover for me."

"Then I arrived in time. It's a wonderful package," she told Adam Boyer.

"She's perfect the way she is," Adam, a tall ex-navy SEAL, all but growled.

Joy just managed not to wince, envying Xandra more than usual. She wished just once she'd heard those words from Brian. Ruthlessly, she banished the thought. She did not need Brian Peterson's stamp of approval on her or the way she chose to live her life.

"Are you all right?" Xandra asked.

Joy forced a smile. "I was just distracted," she said, then centered her attention on Adam. "Tomorrow is Mother's Day and this is what your sons' mother wants. How can you deny her? Besides, Adam, it's a day of pampering *not* of plastic surgery. I promise you'll still recognize her. And since she'll also get a new outfit, you'll have a great excuse to pamper her even more with a lovely dinner afterward. The Black Orchid has an intimate dinner for two up for bid," she hinted. "Remember, Angel Flight helps kids not as lucky as Mark and Luke."

"Oh, all right," Adam conceded, tucking Xandra

against his side. "Let's go place a bid. If we lose I'll still send you to the spa. All right, honey? But they'd better not go cutting your hair. I like it long."

Joy faded away. They had eyes only for each other anyway. Smiling at how fiercely tender Adam had sounded, she moved off toward Meg's nephew, Cole Taggert and his wife CJ on the off-chance she could push the bidding upward. Halfway across the room someone called her name. She turned to find herself looking down at Snow White.

"Linda Haversham," Snow said by way of a reminder of their meeting. As if Joy could forget. Every second of those eye-opening moments were burned into her brain.

"Nice to see you again," Joy said, determined to be kind. After all, what could she say? *I hate your guts, especially because you're so nice!*

"Joy. This is my husband, Rick. Rick this is Joy Lovell. Joy was the pilot Brian was in the plane crash with."

Doctor Haversham, a short, thin runner-type, took her hand and shot her a wicked smile. "I rarely get to see the news but now I understand. Brian's a lucky man." Joy was surprised to see Linda elbow her husband. "Huh?" He blinked. "Uh…I mean…lucky you bought enough time for him to bail out."

Joy didn't want to think about Brian or their time in the preserve. If she did, she'd never get through the night, so she turned again to her purpose for being there, clinging to it like a lifeline. "The day we met your wife she joked about the trials of being a parent. I've suggested to a few husbands that the day at the spa would be an excellent Mother's Day gift."

Even though Linda was perfectly put together, she latched onto the suggestion like a drowning person onto a life preserver. "That sounds like a unique experience. Let's go bid on it," she said, taking Rick Haversham's arm and beginning to pull him toward the auction table.

He allowed himself to be led away but a surprised, "Linda, I bought you a membership to that spa for Christmas," floated back to Joy. She frowned. She must have misheard because that made no sense at all. Why would the woman want a day at a spa she could go to anytime she wanted?

"Joy Lovell?" a voice behind her said. It was a highly cultured voice. She turned to find a gray-haired man in his sixties who was impeccably groomed and wore a dinner jacket that had to have been tailored for him. "I'm Harold Hawkins. I'm chief of staff at Memorial. Doctor Peterson is on staff there, as well as having been a patient."

"I thought he was still hospitalized."

Hawkins frowned and shook his head. "No. And we were not pleased when he signed himself out. It doesn't look good when one of our own refuses sound medical advice. Sends a bad signal."

"Brian signed himself out?" Joy was stunned. That didn't sound at all like by-the-book Brian. "Why would he do that? He must know he needs to do the physical therapy."

"One would assume. I believe it had something to do

with you. I wondered if you would consider using your influence to get him to return for an evaluation. And perhaps you could tell him I didn't mean he wasn't welcome to practice at Memorial."

Joy felt her blood pressure skyrocket. Furious and incredulous, she went on the attack. "You fired him! How could you? He's a talented, gifted surgeon and children love him almost as much as he loves them. Talk about kicking a man when he's down. What kind of doctor are you?"

Dr. Hawkin's chin came up in defense. "He's on staff at two other hospitals, so it isn't as if I'd pulled the rug out from under him. He mentioned that he intended to cut back to one hospital when he went back to work. I'd hoped we would be that hospital. I would like to make amends, but each time I call he cuts me off and tells me he's working on something more important and that he'll get back to me. Honestly, what could be more important than his career?"

"She is," Brian said, suddenly appearing at Joy's side. "And if you will excuse us, I intend to convince her of that."

Chapter Nineteen

Clearly stunned by his sudden appearance, Joy easily let Brian lead her out of the room onto the adjoining terrace. He fought a grin as he considered the idea of spending the coming years finding ways to keep her half a bubble off level. She was much easier to deal with when she was off balance.

Then she turned to face him and the fire in her eyes had him quickly rethinking his plan. At the edge of panic, he wondered exactly who had led whom out of earshot of the other guests.

He looked away from her, determined not to let last-minute misgivings interfere with his strategy. Too much was riding on tonight and a lot of work had gone into making this scheme unfold so seamlessly. It hadn't been easy to gain the cooperation of every person who'd come to Laurel Glen that night. He'd called in markers, begged favors and jokingly promised their firstborn in marriage just to fill those rooms.

Joy's brother had threatened his very existence if the

evening hurt Joy in any way, but Jim had gone ahead and enlisted the aid of his extended family, hoping to help Brian prove his love for Joy. And prove to her that she was perfect just the way she was.

They'd all chipped in and worked like troopers to make this charity event look as if it had taken weeks to put together. Brian knew Meg had been careful to float that impression so Joy wouldn't suspect anything. Disabusing her of that fact was the trickiest part of this whole insane plan. She could get so angry she'd storm away and be done with the whole lot of them, but he'd seen no other way. Worried as he was, Brian was still determined to be truthful. He would not have a lie— even an assumed one—come back to haunt them.

"I'm sorry," he rushed to say now that they were away from the party and it was time to face the music.

She stiffened more when he hadn't thought her back could get any more rigid. "What exactly are you apologizing for this time?" she wanted to know.

Brian raked his hand through his hair, stalling. "It's a…a blanket apology," he hedged, then added, "for whatever you want to apply it to. Just in case. Promise me you won't run away again before we settle several things between us." She opened her mouth and he knew it was to deny that she'd ever run from anything in her life. He covered her lips with his index finger. "Aaah! You disappeared from my hospital room at Memorial and didn't even leave a puff of smoke behind."

He knew he had her there by the way she tipped her chin up and looked away. "I had a lot of work to do at Agape Air."

He believed that to be true but doubted it as the reason she'd suddenly fled his room. "Please come sit down and just talk to me," he said, and ushered her around the corner to an area at the back of the house far from prying eyes. In the center of the wide stone terrace stood a chimenea with a cheerful fire burning in it. There was a semicircle of stone benches in front of the opening that provided a cozy spot for a long overdue talk.

She stopped dead. "This looks awfully preplanned."

He'd worried that the May night would be too cool for her in the sleeveless dress she'd worn, so he had her shawl waiting there. He picked it up off the stone wall where he'd left it and draped it over her shoulders. "We needed to talk so I arranged it with Ross Taggert, or rather Jim did."

Brian sat and looked up at her. Joy didn't move but for the moment he didn't mind. She was so beautiful it took his breath and stuffed it right back down his throat. Her dress had a strong Asian influence and covered her from neck to ankle, with the exception of slits that went only to her knees. It was probably the most modest dress any of the women wore that night but it was utterly alluring to Brian. He was sure that had more to do with the depth of his love than anything else.

He held out his uncasted hand in invitation, thinking he could loop his arm around her shoulders to keep her close. "Please," he all but begged.

"You sound like a four-year-old trying to wheedle a second cookie," she snapped. She did sit, but on a different bench.

Refusing to be baited, he stood, moved to the end of the bench next to hers and straddled it so he faced her. The spring breeze ruffled her short hair and the fire played on her smooth cheeks and glittered in her remote, blue eyes. It was hard to keep from reaching out to her—even though she clearly preferred to be at arm's length—because he wanted to banish that distant look forever. He'd been looking at it for years across rooms.

"It isn't going to work. No matter what rotten things you say to me, I'm not getting mad so stop trying to provoke me. No matter how you try to freeze me out, I'm not going away. I don't want to be saved, Joy," he said with deliberate care, then leaned forward and kissed her on the cheek. Her head snapped around and their gazes locked.

She didn't even pretend not to know what he meant. "Who told you—"

"Shh," he whispered and kissed her lips this time. "I love you," he said against those captivating lips of hers. She turned her head again to face the fire, so he finished his thought a centimeter from her ear. "And I'm not sacrificing our happiness because you have some mistaken idea of what I want and need from you."

He sat back but only a little. "You left my hospital room because somehow or other, Linda intimidated you. How Linda could intimidate a woman of your accomplishments is beyond me but that's what George says happened."

She gritted her teeth. "Uncle George is going to pay. And I didn't say she intimidated me."

"Okay. Let's revisit what happened that day and you

explain it to me in your words. You came to ask what I meant on the ledge and to tell me I had the wrong idea about your desire for children. It was part of our argument years ago. I freely admit I've always seen my future wife as a full-time wife and mother, but I've always thought you weren't planning on kids at all. That subject aside, I find it hard to believe you came there to deliver a message that personal for no reason at all." He waited but she remained stoically silent. "Nothing to say? Then suppose I try to fill in the blanks. I think you came to try to work things out between us but then Linda showed up. You left because you remembered the rest of my sophomoric life plan and you decided it was beyond you."

"Why did you have to come here tonight?" Her voice shook and she clenched her hands in her lap.

Okay, so she could still provoke him and who would ever have thought seeing her in such obvious pain would make him angry. "Because I arranged for you to be here. I arranged the whole night. It was bait. And a test."

The fire exploded back into her eyes and he was glad. He wanted her mad at him in that moment because he was mad at both of them. They'd wasted so much time already.

"Was it a pass-fail grade or were you and your co-conspirators grading me in increments?" she demanded.

"I wouldn't know. You're the one who has to do the grading. How would you say you did tonight?"

She stared at him as if one of them—most likely him—had lost their mind. "I don't understand."

"Basically, I got Meg to throw you to your wolves. You have a lot of misconceptions but this was one I couldn't let you have even if we never see each other after tonight. First, I don't care if you ever volunteer for a charity committee. Twelve years have not only changed me, they've changed the world. The point of this party is that you can handle anything. If something was important enough, you could do it. You just did. Not, I want to add, that there's any way you could adversely impact my professional life."

She arched her eyebrow and smirked. "Apparently, I'm the reason you got kicked off the staff of Memorial. That self-important, chief-of-staff person I was talking to seemed to want you back but then I told him off so who knows, now."

Brian grinned, remembering the look on Hawkins' face from across the room. "He never had the power to suspend me for checking myself out. I didn't even listen. Thank you, though. It's nice to have you in my cheering section. And I'd sincerely like to keep you there. You didn't reciprocate, by the way."

She blinked—off balance again. "Reciprocate?"

He looked at the ground then back up at her. Time for even more honesty. "I said I love you. You didn't say it back. That hurts, Joy. A lot. The last time I said it, you admitted you loved me, too, but you still said goodbye. That hurt, too."

"Look, I do love you and I don't want to hurt you but we want different things."

"And I don't want to hurt you, but I have. Years ago I acted as if those things mattered more than *you*. They don't matter. You do." Brian gently turned her face to his. He left his palm resting against her cheek, his thumb caressing her face. "I want you for my wife. Whatever that means."

Joy looked away from his beloved face. Afraid to hope. Afraid to see the dream die in his gaze. "But I can't be the wife you want. You admitted you've always wanted a stay-at-home wife and mother for you and your children. I could try to be that person but I don't want to try because I know I'd be miserable. Then I'd make you miserable. You called it right when you said Agape has been like my child. I couldn't abandon it or the men and women who depend on me for a living anymore than I could abandon my own children."

"And I'm no longer asking you to."

"Then what do you want? You said compromise. You've already said you don't care if I join those charity committees."

"You have more important ways to spend your time."

She threw up her hands and turned more fully to face him. "Then I'd have to give up Agape. It's a great choice you've left me with. Either I'm miserable with you or miserable without you."

"But Agape Air *is* the more important thing you do with your time. Dreams change, Joy. Mine has. George told me about the extra office next to yours that you can use as a nursery and playroom. And Memorial has a great day care right there. I could take our kids there on days you're tied up until they're ready to go to school. I can even have lunch with them."

She remembered his reaction when she'd told him to

parachute out of the crippled Cessna without her. "Then what's my concession in this? Flying?"

He shook his head and smiled sadly, but it faded quickly. "I'm not asking you not to fly. All I'm asking is to stop acting as if you're unbreakable," his voice cracked, and what she saw in his eyes broke her heart all over again. He was terrified for her and he confirmed it when he continued. "Just quit winding up on the evening news. How many community commendations for risking your neck do you need hanging on your wall, anyway?"

He shook his head and ran his good hand through his hair. "I haven't been able to sleep since we got back. Do you know why? I keep reliving those minutes in the plane when you said you were flying on to try to land the plane after I jumped. Only this time I let you have your way and I then I'm floating to earth and watch you smash into that cliff. Then I'm suddenly rappelling down the cliff to find you dead in the cockpit. I wake up in a cold sweat, then, screaming your name."

Joy turned to him. Her hand slid over his unbandaged hand and held it. "I've only taken one flight since the crash, Bri. A puddle jump to Pittsburgh. I meant it when I told you I don't have a death wish. I never intended to continue taking chances once there were others who depended on me. But since I didn't have anyone in my life, I've tried to help save the lives of people who did." She took a deep breath. Could this really be happening? She ran a quick mental checklist. Had they really managed to comprise on all the issues keeping them apart?

"You'd really be okay with all of this? It feels as if

you're doing all the giving. I don't want you to wind up hating me."

He smiled but it was tinged with sadness. "I love you. How could I hate you for being you? I'm so sorry for ever making you think I would. Joy, I want *you* for my wife. Not some conjured set of statistics I dreamed up when I was an idiot fifteen-year-old. I can hire a housekeeper, a cook and the occasional babysitter. But *you* are one of a kind. I want you to be my partner. My love."

He slid to his knee and she had to blink away tears just to see him. And she blinked really hard because she wasn't going to miss even a second of this. "Will you marry me?" he said and pulled a platinum and diamond solitaire out of his sling.

He looked up at her, an embarrassed grin pulling at his lips, and she knew exactly what he was remembering. Another ring. One expensive, gaudy nightmare of a ring with too many strings.

"See, I really know you now. The wedding bands are just as plain. Come on, Joyful, put me out of my misery."

Joy felt the tears she'd been holding back spill over and run down her cheeks. "I love you. And yes. I'll marry you."

And then Brian was there sharing the bench, drying her tears and laughing. "You're not supposed to cry, Joyful, but if you want to, you go right ahead. Then we'll go turn that benefit into an engagement party."

Thinking of all the people he'd had to get there, she asked, "Why'd you go through all that trouble?"

He just smiled gently and kissed her. "When I was running around this week like a nut my brother asked me the same thing. I'll tell you what I told him. Because I have Joy in my heart."

Dear Reader,

Brian and Joy's story has been floating around in my brain ever since I met the Peterson and Lovell families while writing my second Love Inspired novel. This was a book about paths. I wanted to show how two people could start out on the same path, be raised nearly side by side, need to walk a different path and yet still be perfect for one another. The Lord has plans and a path He's chosen for each of us to take through this world. His plan in *Joy in His Heart* was that these two very different people, regardless of their rocky pasts, were meant to be together. I truly believe that though the Lord is patient, He will get our attention if we aren't following His direction. He gave Brian and Joy twelve years before literally knocking them out of the sky so they'd have to talk to each other and follow the path He'd chosen for them.

We must always remember it's supposed to be His plan. Give your life into His hands, and you'll know you're walking the right path.

I love hearing from my readers at kate_welsh@earthlink.net. I regret I can only answer letters accompanied with a stamped, self-addressed envelope when you write me via snail mail through Love Inspired.

God Bless

Kate Welsh

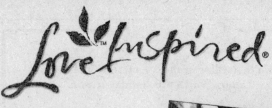

Love Inspired SUSPENSE
RIVETING INSPIRATIONAL ROMANCE

YULETIDE PERIL

by Irene Brand

Hoping to start a new life for herself and her younger sister, Janice Reid moves to Stanton, West Virginia, to take possession of a house her uncle left her. But Janice soon becomes the target of harassment and threats, which threaten both her newfound security and her developing relationship with Lance Gordon.

"Irene Brand pens a heartwarming romance with a strong message."
—*Romantic Times BOOKclub*

Steeple Hill®

Don't miss *Yuletide Peril*
On sale December 2005
Available at your favorite retail outlet.

LARGER PRINT BOOKS!

2 FREE LARGER PRINT NOVELS PLUS A FREE MYSTERY GIFT

Larger print novels are now available...

YES! Please send me 2 FREE LARGER PRINT Love Inspired® novels and my FREE mystery gift. After receiving them, if I don't wish to receive any more books, I can return the shipping statement marked "cancel." If I don't cancel, I will receive 4 brand-new novels every month and be billed just $4.24 per book in the U.S., or $4.99 per book in Canada, plus 25¢ shipping and handling per book and applicable taxes, if any*. That's a savings of over 20% off the cover price! I understand that accepting the 2 free books and gift places me under no obligation to buy anything. I can always return a shipment and cancel at any time. Even if I never buy another book from Steeple Hill, the two free books and gift are mine to keep forever.

121 IDN D733 321 IDN D74F

Name	(PLEASE PRINT)	
Address		Apt.
City	State/Prov.	Zip/Postal Code

Signature (if under 18, a parent or guardian must sign)

Order online at www.LoveInspiredBooks.com

Or mail to Steeple Hill Reader Service™:

IN U.S.A.	IN CANADA
3010 Walden Ave.	P.O. Box 609
P.O. Box 1867	Fort Erie, Ontario
Buffalo, NY 14240-1867	L2A 5X3

Are you a current Love Inspired subscriber and want to receive the larger print edition?

Call 1-800-221-5011 today!

* Terms and prices subject to change without notice. NY residents add applicable sales tax. Canadian residents will be charged applicable provincial taxes and GST. This offer is limited to one order per household. All orders subject to approval. Credit or debit balances in a customer's account(s) may be offset by any other outstanding balance owed by or to the customer.

LILP005

TITLES AVAILABLE NEXT MONTH

Don't miss these four stories in December

BLESSED VOWS by Jillian Hart
The McKaslin Clan

Jake McCall's sudden proposal surprised Rachel McKaslin—they hadn't been dating that long. The handsome military man had promised to care for his orphaned niece but was being deployed unexpectedly. Rachel's love for the child made marrying her the perfect solution. Would time apart make Jake see the true treasure he left behind?

PAST SECRETS, PRESENT LOVE by Lois Richer
Tiny Blessings

Private investigator Ross Van Zandt delivered some shocking news to Kelly Young. Now, as the director of the Tiny Blessings adoption agency tries to come to terms with the revelation, she finds herself falling for the handsome sleuth. But Ross is keeping a secret that could tear them apart....

SUGAR PLUMS FOR DRY CREEK by Janet Tronstad

When the residents of Dry Creek heard newcomer Lizette Baker's name, they expected a bakery from the young businesswoman, not a dance studio. Lizette hoped her Christmas production of *The Nutcracker* would win them over, yet when she met her students' handsome guardian, her visions of sugar plums began to turn into dreams of love....

A PERFECT LOVE by Lenora Worth
Texas Hearts

Hoping a trip would help her recharge, world-weary city girl Summer Maxwell returned to her small hometown. When her car broke down on the way, landscaper Mack Riley came to her rescue, and sparks flew. Yet Summer's unresolved family problems and Mack's troubled past could put the brakes on their connection.

LICNM1105